15 Leadership Principles and Ronald Reagan

Use Them to Change Your World

[signature: Larry W. Dennis]

Larry W. Dennis, Sr.

with Kathryn Hickok

[signature: Kathryn Hickok]

Rising Tide Publishing
Portland, Oregon

15 Leadership Principles and Ronald Reagan
Use Them to Change Your World

Forward Copyright Margaret Thatcher. Reproduced by permission of
www.margaretthatcher.org, the official website of the Margaret Thatcher
Foundation.

Rising Tide Publishing
36280 N.E. Wilsonville Rd.
Newberg, Oregon 97132
E-mail: turbo@turboleadershipsystems.com
www.turboleadershipsystems.com

Cover Design: Richard Ferguson
Editing, Design, Typographics: Kathryn Hickok

First Printing 2007

Other books by Larry W. Dennis, Sr.

Empowering Leadership
How to Turbo Charge You: Six Steps to Tap Your True Potential
In Formation: How to Gain the 71% Advantage
Making Moments Matter: 89 Tools for Taking Charge of Your Life
Repeat Business: 6 Steps to Superior Customer Service
The Great Baseball Cap
Motorcycle Meditations: A Vision Quest to Alaska

Dedication

This book is dedicated to those human spirits on islands, peninsulas, and continents who remain today in captivity. May some brave, courageous leader hold the torch of freedom high and guide them to liberty.

Table of Contents

Forward

Former Prime Minister Margaret Thatcher's
Eulogy of President Ronald Reagan
June 11, 2004

We have lost a great president, a great American, and a great man, and I have lost a dear friend. In his lifetime, Ronald Reagan was such a cheerful and invigorating presence that it was easy to forget what daunting historic tasks he set himself. He sought to mend America's wounded spirit, to restore the strength of the free world, and to free the slaves of communism. These were causes hard to accomplish and heavy with risk, yet they were pursued with almost a lightness of spirit, for Ronald Reagan also embodied another great cause, what Arnold Bennett once called "the great cause of cheering us all up." His policies had a freshness and optimism that won converts from every class and every nation, and ultimately, from the very heart of the "evil empire."

Yet his humor often had a purpose beyond humor. In the terrible hours after the attempt on his life, his easy jokes gave reassurance to an anxious world. They were evidence that in the aftermath of terror and in the midst of hysteria one great heart at least remained sane and jocular. They were truly grace under pressure. And perhaps they signified grace of a deeper kind. Ronnie himself certainly believed that he had been given back his life for a purpose. As he told a priest after his recovery, "Whatever time I've got left now belongs to the big fella upstairs." And surely, it is hard to deny that Ronald Reagan's life was providential when we look at what he achieved in the eight years that followed.

Others prophesied the decline of the West. He inspired America and its allies with renewed faith in their mission of freedom.

Others saw only limits to growth. He transformed a stagnant economy into an engine of opportunity.

Others hoped, at best, for an uneasy cohabitation with the Soviet Union. He won the Cold War, not only without firing a shot, but also by inviting enemies out of their fortress and turning them into friends.

I cannot imagine how any diplomat or any dramatist could improve on his words to Mikhail Gorbachev at the Geneva summit. "Let

10

me tell you why it is we distrust you." Those words are candid and tough, and they cannot have been easy to hear. But they are also a clear invitation to a new beginning and a new relationship that would be rooted in trust.

We live today in the world that Ronald Reagan began to reshape with those words. It is a very different world, with different challenges and new dangers. All in all, however, it is one of greater freedom and prosperity, one more hopeful than the world he inherited on becoming president.

As Prime Minister, I worked closely with Ronald Reagan for eight of the most important years of all our lives. We talked regularly, both before and after his presidency, and I've had time and cause to reflect on what made him a great president.

Ronald Reagan knew his own mind. He had firm principles and, I believe, right ones. He expounded them clearly. He acted upon them decisively. When the world threw problems at the White House, he was not baffled or disorientated or overwhelmed.

He knew almost instinctively what to do.

When his aides were preparing option papers for his decision, they were able to cut out entire rafts of proposals that they knew the old man would never wear. When his allies came under Soviet or domestic pressure, they could

11

look confidently to Washington for firm leadership, and when his enemies tested American resolve, they soon discovered that his resolve was firm and unyielding.

Yet his ideas, so clear, were never simplistic. He saw the many sides of truth. Yes, he warned that the Soviet Union had an insatiable drive for military power and territorial expansion, but he also sensed that it was being eaten away by systemic failures impossible to reform. Yes, he did not shrink from denouncing Moscow's evil empire, but he realized that a man of good will might nonetheless emerge from within its dark corridors.

So the president resisted Soviet expansion and pressed down on Soviet weakness at every point until the day came when communism began to collapse beneath the combined weight of those pressures and its own failures. And when a man of good will did emerge from the ruins, President Reagan stepped forward to shake his hand and to offer sincere cooperation.

Nothing was more typical of Ronald Reagan than that large-hearted magnanimity, and nothing was more American.

Therein lies perhaps the final explanation of his achievements. Ronald Reagan carried the American people with him in his great endeavours because there was perfect sympathy between them. He and they loved America and what it stands for: freedom and opportunity for ordinary people.

As an actor in Hollywood's golden age, he helped to make the American dream live for millions all over the globe. His own life was a fulfillment of that dream. He never succumbed to the embarrassment some people feel about an honest expression of love of country. He was able to say "God bless America" with equal fervor in public and in private. And so he was able to call confidently upon his fellow countrymen to make sacrifices for America and to make sacrifices for those who look to America for hope and rescue.

With the lever of American patriotism, he lifted up the world. And so today, the world—in Prague, in Budapest, in Warsaw and Sofia, in Bucharest, in Kiev, and in Moscow itself, the world mourns the passing of the great liberator and echoes his prayer: God bless America.

Ronald Reagan's life was rich not only in public achievement, but also in private happiness. Indeed, his public achievements were rooted in his private happiness.

The great turning point of his life was his meeting and marriage with Nancy. On that, we have the plain testimony of a loving and grateful husband. "Nancy came along and saved my soul."

We share her grief today, but we also share her pride and the grief and pride of Ronnie's children. For the final years of his life, Ronnie's mind was clouded by illness. That cloud has now lifted. He is himself again, more himself than at any time on this Earth, for we may be sure that the Big Fellow upstairs never forgets those who remember him. And as the last journey of this faithful pilgrim took him beyond the sunset, and as heaven's morning broke, I like to think, in the words of Bunyan, that "all the trumpets sounded on the other side."

We here still move in twilight, but we have one beacon to guide us that Ronald Reagan never had. We have his example. Let us give thanks today for a life that achieved so much for all of God's children.

Introduction

On Saturday, June 5, 2004, I had been working in the yard with my crew, building the foundation for a new gazebo. I was making a run to town to get the balance of the materials I needed to complete the foundation. As I drove down the road, I heard an announcement on the radio that Ronald Reagan died. Without a thought, I instantly said, "Oh no!" and cried for the next several minutes. I had never had this kind of experience before in my life. I never would have anticipated that I would react this way to the news of President Reagan's death. The sense of loss I felt is hard to express, and I found myself trying to understand why I responded to his death the way I did.

Thinking about what President Reagan meant to me, to our country, and to the world in which we live led me to write this book. Based on over three decades of training managers to be empowering leaders, I have written about maximizing your potential and leading others to help them maximize their potential. Certainly, Ronald Reagan is a quintessential example of both. The challenge in writing this book was not finding examples of Reagan's empowering leadership style; it was deciding which of the vast examples to include.

Speaking at Ronald Reagan's funeral on June 11, an emotional George H. W. Bush said Reagan "believed in America, so he made it his shining city on a hill. He believed in freedom, so he acted on behalf of its values and ideals....As his vice president for eight years, I learned more from Ronald Reagan than from anyone I encountered in all my years in public life. I learned kindness—we all did. I also learned courage—the nation did."

The world is different because of Ronald Reagan. President Reagan was an empowering leader with the vision and courage to change the world. At the time of his inauguration in 1981, nearly 80% of the world's population lived under Communist regimes. The free nations were not sure there was anything they could do to stop the expansion of Communism. Some argued there was not even any reason why Communism should be stopped. Domestically, America faced double-digit inflation and interest rates. Unemployment was rising. Economic growth was stagnant. Many were cynical about the future of America, her role in the world, and the ability of public officials to demonstrate principled and effective leadership.

Today, almost twenty-five years later, there is more freedom, more liberty, than ever before in human history. The expansion of Communism was not just stopped; the Cold War was won. By the end of the Reagan decade, the Soviet Union was history. The Berlin Wall was down. There was one Germany. Eastern Europe was free. The American economy had recovered; inflation had slowed. Reagan proved that the presidency, in the hands of an empowering leader, is still strong and that the American people are still great.

In her eulogy of the president, Lady Margaret Thatcher said, "He inspired America and its allies with renewed faith in our mission of freedom." Lady Thatcher dedicated her 2002 book *Statecraft: Strategies for a Changing World* to Ronald Reagan, "[t]o whom the world owes so much."

Former New York City Mayor Rudolph Giuliani recently said President Reagan was "a statesman of the first order—persuasive, disarming, instinctive. He inspired America and the entire world with the clarity of his vision and his sense of direction and purpose."[1] The key to Ronald Reagan's greatness was his positive, empowering leadership. He believed in the greatness of America and had the ability and the enthusiasm to lead from his high ideals.

On September 1, 2004, Reagan's son Michael said, "Throughout his life, his belief in you and me—the American people—never ever wavered."[2] Reagan didn't wait for situations to change or for success to be achieved before offering the nation words of encouragement and praise. He reminded us again and again of the uniqueness of America, of our proud history, and of our potential for future greatness. He believed that America is a "shining city on a hill," a beacon of freedom and hope for the whole world.

Reagan understood the importance of constantly striving to make the ideal the reality. He believed that constantly challenging people to bring the best out of themselves has results, that saying so really can make it so. When he met the new general secretary of the Soviet Union, he reminded Mikhail Gorbachev that the two of them had the power to change U.S.-Soviet relations forever. He challenged Gorbachev to work for change, and Gorbachev did.

"He was an authentic person and a great person," Gorbachev once said of Reagan. "If someone else had been in his place, I don't know if what happened would have happened."[3] On June 11, the last Communist leader of the

Union of Soviet Socialist Republics sat behind Reagan's grandchildren in the National Cathedral in Washington, D.C., paying silent tribute to a rival who had become a friend.

A quarter-century ago, when Reagan was first elected president, who would have thought this was possible? "The Iron Curtain came down for good," Reagan once said, "and the special joy I felt was that the answer came in my lifetime."[4]

The Reverend Daniel Coughlin, chaplain of the House of Representatives, said of Reagan: "With his style and grace he made it seem easy. With his compassion and sense of timing he brought strength of character to the nation and enkindled hope in a darkened world."[5]

Reagan understood the importance of listening, of being interested in the concerns of others, of building people up by seeing their point of view and empowering them to put their plans into action.

A man of legendary wit, Reagan was big enough to poke fun at himself, to soften a rejoinder with humor, and to choose the positive response over the negative.

A keen negotiator, Reagan knew that one gets the best deal by avoiding destructive arguments and dogmatic declarations and by beginning from points of agreement. He was tough, but he gave the other party space to save face with dignity. He could take the 80% and come back for the rest later. Former Secretary of State Howard Baker claimed that in negotiation, "it was his idealism and his endless strength and courage that put America and the world on the road to lasting peace."[6]

Reagan would compromise on the details but never on the principle. "We can never go wrong if we do what is morally right...,"[7] he said. He had the courage to take responsibility for mistakes—his own and those of his administration.

He dared to appeal to other people's noble motives, to spark their imaginations with vivid descriptions of how things are and of how things can be. Former Attorney General Edwin Meese III wrote that while people called Reagan "The Great Communicator," "some never grasped that it was *what* he was communicating that gave his message its political impact."[8]

Reagan's greatness as an empowering leader was not the work of a day. His whole life prepared him for his presidency. From his boyhood home of Dixon, Illinois, through his days in California as a movie star and then as governor of one of the most populous and diverse states in the Union, to his emergence as a political figure of national stature, and through his historic presidency, Ronald Reagan proved himself a man of visionary leadership and

20

personal integrity. His critics and political opponents often acknowledge both his leadership abilities and personal charm.

Ronald Reagan believed that anyone— everyone—can change their world. Everyone can be an empowering leader. What it takes is the belief that people can affect their own destinies and those of their team and organization. Reagan was not a fatalist; he was an optimist. He believed that one person's step is one step to changing the world for the better. He took the steps he could and changed his world. Take the steps you can, and you will change yourself, your team, your organization, your world.

"We did more than just pass through," President Reagan said after leaving office, "we got America moving again. We breathed new life into our economy and put more people to work than ever before in history. We rebuilt our military strength, and brought the world a little closer together in peace. But above all, more than anything else, we got America to stand tall again. And, you know, I'd like to think maybe that's the thing I'm proudest of."[9]

As we explore how Reagan influenced the world, we can learn from his example and see how we, too, can influence our world. Let Ronald Reagan show you how you can be an empowering leader.

Leadership Principle 1

"I never thought of myself as a great man, just a man committed to great ideas....History has taught me that this is what sets America apart—not to remake the world in our image, but to inspire people everywhere with a sense of their own boundless possibilities. There's no question I am an idealist, which is another way of saying I am an American."

Ronald Reagan[1]

Lead From High Ideals

Just prior to his famous speech at the Brandenburg Gate in 1987, Ronald Reagan crossed over into East Berlin. He paused to read the graffiti spray-painted on the Soviet side of the Berlin Wall: "This wall will fall. Beliefs become reality." Reagan was touched by this simple declaration of the ultimate triumph of freedom.[2] That freedom can and should prevail was the heart of Ronald Reagan's vision for America and for the world. He believed in the power of high ideals to change history.

In 1977 Reagan told Richard Allen, later to become his national security advisor in the White House, "Some people think I'm simplistic, but there's a difference between being simplistic and being simple. My theory of the Cold War is that we win and they lose. What do you think of that?"

Allen asked if Reagan meant it. "Of course I mean it," Reagan replied. "I just said it."[3] Reagan showed by his actions as president of the United States that leadership is a choice to be made, not a position to be held. He led with moral authority because his word was good. Meaning what he said required putting his words into action.

Ronald Reagan changed the landscape of America and the world because he had a compelling vision he successfully communicated and staunchly championed. Leading from high ideals, Reagan brought us back to the fundamental and unique values of liberty that distinguish us as a nation. You, as an empowering leader, also must lead from high ideals if you want to make an impact and change your world. Your goal is to create a unique approach to quality, leadership, innovation, trust, teamwork, customer-focused service, and organization alignment. People enthusiastically follow leaders who do and say the right thing in the right way.

Most organizations have a mission, vision, and values statement in place. Your mission is why your organization exists, the difference you make in the world. It can be compared to the United States of America's Declaration of Independence. Your vision statement creates a mental picture of the desired future state of your organization. It takes all key stakeholders into account and is a motivation to the reader. A vision statement is similar to our U.S. Constitution. Your values—the principles that guide your relationships, behavior, and decisions as an organization—correspond to the Bill of Rights. Your organization may also have a credo or slogan prominently printed on your business cards, letterhead, ads, and vehicles, just as "In God We Trust" is found on our money.

Your job as an empowering leader is to talk about and keep your organization focused on your mission, vision, and values. If your team members forget the vision, everything they do has less meaning and is ineffective. When your team remembers the purpose, they have a beacon to illuminate their path; and all they do derives meaning and power from your intention.

You continually refer the team back to these ideals which are the crafters of your organization's culture. These documents become the framers of who you are, what you do, and why you do it. They become the ultimate authority within your organization.

As your team begins to understand that they are to be guided by these ideals, not by a controlling manager or rigid policies and procedures, they become motivated to give their best. As you allow these ideals to be the ultimate authority, you satisfy your associates' deepest needs. Your associates are aching to make a difference, hungry to make a contribution, and yearning to be recognized. They need to leave a legacy.

You will be successful as an empowering leader—you will have people follow you enthusiastically—only when they think they are making a difference. They must feel they are contributing to a worthy cause and know their efforts are recognized and their needs ("what's in it for me?") are being met. If you think they should figure out for themselves the guiding principles of your organization, you have misunderstood your job. If you grow tired of talking about your organization's mission, vision, and values (your guiding principles), you have grown tired of your job.

Certainly, you are a working manager—you "have the tool belt on" a good part of the day. Your work tasks may take up to 80% of your time. You may be using so much time on the "trivial many" work tasks that could be delegated or create little value for your organization that you have little time for the "vital few" activities which constitute your most important role as an empowering leader. These "vital few" tasks make up the important part of the day when you interact with your team, referring them back to the mission, vision, and values of your organization.

Make your ideals the framework of all your communication. Empowering leaders learn to talk in a way that *motivates people*. What do empowering leaders talk about to win the hearts of their team members? Empowering leaders talk about what is important, where we are headed, and what we stand for.

Inspire people to overcome the inclination to play it safe. Mission, vision, and values provide the context for tough decisions, changes of course, risks you take, downsizing, upsizing, outsourcing, streamlining, capital investment, acquisitions, investiture, and expansion. When you stay focused on your ideals, you will keep your team on the right track.

———

Michael Reagan said of his father: "He spoke of renewal and hope; of defeating Communism, not accommodating it; of economically revitalizing America with lower taxes and less government; and of...faith. When it was unfashionable and corny, he spoke of the values that had made America great and noble and wealthy, and of how we must return to those values. He infused millions—both in the United States and around the world—with new hope and a new spirit."[4]

Reagan had a core; he wasn't an "empty suit." Former congressman and presidential candidate Jack Kemp said of Reagan: "Most politicians talk about policies and the changing issues of the day. Ronald Reagan talked about principles—deeply held beliefs. The difference is profound. Policies shift with the breeze of public opinion, but principles are anchors, even in a storm."[5] As Reagan himself said, "Most often it's not how handsomely or eloquently you say something, but the fact that your words mean something."[6]

In your role as an empowering leader, you too can call your team to record-setting performance, market dominance, double-digit growth and profit. Your organization may have experienced setbacks of many kinds: loss of customers, loss of dealers, new competition, serious accidents, equipment failures, accelerating costs, suppliers who have let you down. This is the nature of business; and this is why you must be the stabilizing force of your organization, just as Ronald Reagan was for the nation.

Our guiding principles—our mission, vision, and values—remind us that we are bigger than the obstacles we encounter.

Empowering leaders embolden the team to believe that they are more than equal to the task at hand. When we stand together, we can overcome any obstacle to meet and exceed our goals.

———

A poll during the Reagan administration showed that 70% of Americans could name at least one of the president's most important priorities, compared with 15-45% during the previous four administrations.[7] Reagan worked hard to convey his message. He said, "I usually start with a joke or story to catch the audience's attention; then I tell them what I am going to tell them, I tell them, and then I tell them what I just told them."[8] Reagan's team reinforced his vision by circulating his speeches among the White House staff to remind them of the mission, vision, and values of his administration.[9] Reagan knew that repetition is the key to memory, and his vision as a leader would not get out without constant repetition.

Ronald Reagan knew what he stood for and proved it by expressing his ideals in a clear, concise, cohesive way. He had the ability to communicate an inspiring vision to the hearts and minds of his listeners. He harnessed the power of mission, vision, and values to motivate the nation, restore lost hope, encourage and motivate beyond cynicism and doubt to faith and courage.

Can your team, from the office to the dock, recite your mission, vision, and values? Do they have line of sight—can they see the connection—between their work tasks and the mission of the organization? If not, you run the risk of losing the heart of your team.

Nothing is more important for you as an empowering leader than to know what you stand for. Until you can successfully articulate what you stand for, you really do not know your own principles. When your message leads from ideals and a clearly communicated set of values, others will join in, rally around, and support the cause. You will have won their hearts.

———

Reagan's ideals and the ability to articulate them brought him to the presidency. Richard Wirthlin, deputy director of strategy and planning for the 1980 Reagan campaign, said that Reagan won the election because "he had a sense of vision of America that provided a frame of reference for the strategy that gave us a consistent and directed thrust to the campaign right from the beginning...."[10]

Having achieved the highest office in

America, Reagan led from his ideals. "Whether we agree with him or not," said Democratic Senator Ted Kennedy, "Ronald Reagan was an effective president. He stood for a set of ideas..., he meant them, and he wrote most of them not only into public law but into national consciousness."[11] Sam Donaldson of ABC News found Reagan to be an outstanding leader where his ideals were concerned: "Where I had disagreements with him, it was about policies I thought were wrong, but I sure knew what they were."[12]

Actor and Reagan friend Charlton Heston recalled that Reagan enjoyed laying out his vision. Heston's memory of the 1984 election was "not that [Reagan] had won by so much," but that he loved speaking about his vision, the message he was trying to get across to the voters. "It was the most fun he could imagine; to go out and campaign and say to people, 'Let me tell you why I want you to vote for me and what my vision is for the country.' Of course, he articulated that vision very, very well. He loved it. In fact, when we got off the plane that day in November 1984, he looked as if he could have started the whole thing over again."[13]

Managers talk about policies and procedures, rules and regulations—technical information about the nature of the competition and the market. They often are experts in their areas from years of experience and specialized training. Empowering leaders talk about the context, not just the content—they focus on people. The context is made up of the vision: principles of integrity, attentive customer service, communication, maximization of resources, return on investment, industry leadership and breakthroughs.

This is the mission statement of your organization, your team's own Declaration of Independence. Content—the details (the concrete steps to attaining your goal)—may be better developed by those on the ground closest to the work. The bottom line is produced by the front line.

Markets change, products change, competitors change, the economy changes. Sometimes even the fundamental products that a company brings to market change. What never changes are the values of your organization's culture. Empowering leaders constantly bring the focus of their team back to the mission, vision, and values of the organization.

———

The first time Reagan laid out his principles before a national audience was his televised speech "A Time for Choosing," given on behalf of presidential candidate Barry

Goldwater. This landmark speech made Reagan a figure of national stature, setting the stage for him to run for governor of California and later for the presidency.

"A Time for Choosing," also called "The Speech," was the most successful political speech to that day, raising eight million dollars for the Goldwater campaign.[14] Goldwater lost in a landslide, but a star was born. Reagan, the man who really galvanized Americans in 1964, was elected governor of California two years later and president of the United States in 1980.

In these famous passages from "The Speech," Reagan began to emerge as a national leader. Speaking with conviction and courage, he outlined the context, the vision, the mission:

"I am going to talk of controversial things. I make no apology for this.

"It's time we asked ourselves if we still know the freedoms intended for us by the Founding Fathers....

"This idea that government was beholden to the people, that it had no other source of power, is still the newest, most unique idea in all the long history of man's relation to man. This is the issue...: whether we believe in our capacity for self-government or whether we abandon the American Revolution and confess that a little intellectual elite in a far-distant capital can plan our lives for us better than we can plan them ourselves....

"They say the world has become too complex for simple answers. They are wrong. There are no easy answers, but there are simple answers. We must have the courage to do what we know is morally right....

"You and I have a rendezvous with destiny. We will preserve for our children this, the last best hope of man on earth, or we will sentence them to take the first step into a thousand years of darkness. If we fail, at least let our children and our children's children say of us we justified our brief moment here. We did all that could be done."[15]

Empowering leaders are optimistic. They see the world from the perspective of how things can be done, not why things cannot be done. Their optimism is not diminished by the difficulties of the moment. Albert Einstein said that imagination is more important than facts. Empowering leaders move forward confident in the truth of what is possible—the truth that when people are fully aligned and engaged, they can overcome seemingly insurmountable obstacles and set new records.

———

As president, Ronald Reagan had the vision to be optimistic that America could and would prevail over the challenges of the late twentieth century. Among his visionary proposals was the Strategic Defense Initiative (SDI), a program to develop technology which would enable countries to defend themselves against the threat of nuclear warfare. Reagan believed that Americans have the ingenuity to invent a working missile defense system to make the nuclear threat obsolete. He foresaw that the Soviet Union would be unable to compete—technologically and economically— with America in an arms race. He had the courageous idealism to stand his ground on SDI, knowing that Soviet opposition to the project was based on fear that America had the capability to succeed and the USSR did not.

In his book *With Reagan*, Reagan advisor and Attorney General Ed Meese wrote that in upholding his vision of SDI, Reagan "took on a whole array of formidable opponents: the arms control establishment..., some elements of the military, liberal Democrats in Congress, pragmatists within the Republican party, and so on....

"...Far from being manipulated, programmed, swayed, or meekly argued out of his position, the President persevered for what he believed, battled for his policy positions, and made the hard decisions that only he could make."[16]

Reagan knew that a successful SDI program would give the United States the competitive advantage over the Soviet Union in the Cold War. Former Secretary of Defense Caspar Weinberger has said that Reagan's "policy initiatives are what won the cold war."[17]

Leaders take risks on unproven technology; they take the risk of pioneering. Consider how IBM has gone from a typewriter and mainframe computer manufacturer to a company that now does business consulting and research and offers personal computing services, software, and storage systems. Rubbermaid began with a rubber dustpan in 1933 and now produces kitchen utensils, organizational bins, cleaning tools, thermal containers, and more. General Electric's production, which began with light bulbs and electric household appliances, now includes jet engines and telecommunication software. The U.S. government installed GE's innovative advanced explosives detection equipment at the Statue of Liberty, enabling the famous monument to reopen with enhanced security in August 2004.

Any change you initiate that has the potential for market growth, improved profits, and competitive advantage will be accompanied by risk. You will be criticized and second-guessed. "Going along" with the status quo is not the leadership your organization wants and needs. When you have the vision and the courage to lead effectively, others will follow you and you will win.

———

Ronald Reagan showed toughness in sticking to principle on the domestic front early in his administration. In 1981 the Professional Air Traffic Controllers Organization (PATCO) went on strike. It is illegal for public sector unions to strike, and a PATCO strike particularly endangered national security. Even though PATCO was one of only a few unions to support Reagan in the 1980 presidential campaign, Reagan took a hard line on the strike. He set a deadline for PATCO to obey the law and then fired employees who refused to comply. Many credit this incident with winning Reagan the respect of the Russians, who were watching to see what kind of man—what kind of leader—the new president was. Wrote Professor Richard Pipes, "It showed them a man who, when aroused, will go to the limit to back up his principles."[18]

As leaders, we are being watched more closely by more eyes than we realize. Each case, every call, affects the larger picture—the cultural environment. There are no isolated acts. Every decision has consequences. Acting on your ideals makes you strong, builds confidence, and leads others to respect you. Exercising empowering leadership results in decisive action, innovation, and competitive advantage. Dare to take risks and stick with your principles, the forward-looking vision of your organization.

———

Reagan boldly championed his ideals. Reagan was called "The Great Communicator," and certainly he was. One of the most fundamental skills of leadership is communication. What makes a great communicator, even more importantly than communication skills, is a heartfelt message. "[S]ome never grasped," wrote Ed Meese, "that it was *what* he was communicating that gave his message its political impact."[19]

In his book *How Ronald Reagan Changed My Life*, former Reagan speechwriter Peter Robinson wrote: "[Reagan had] spent years speaking out on issues even when he'd had no reason to believe anything he said would ever make a difference....And even once he'd become President, Reagan had never quite been able to tell what effect his words might have. He'd admitted as much a few years after leaving office when he remarked that he'd never expected the Berlin Wall to come down as soon as it had....As he'd overruled the State Department and the National Security Council to deliver the Berlin Wall address, all Reagan had known for certain was what he'd told [chief of staff] Kenneth Duberstein in the limousine on the way to the wall itself: 'It's the right thing to do.'

"...I've [learned from Reagan] that even when I have no idea whether anyone is ever listening, which, of course, is most of the time, sticking up for my beliefs is its own reward."[20]

Empowering leaders continually refer back to the mission, vision, and values of the organization, no matter what they are involved in, whether it is firing or hiring, delegating or promoting. The wise empowering leader will find a way to refer to the organization's ideals in at least six important conversations a day.

No matter what your position, you represent your team. When you are asked your opinion in meetings, performance reviews, or plans, this is one more opportunity to reference your high ideals. When you speak from principles, you speak with conviction. When you speak with conviction, you prepare yourself for greater responsibility.

As an empowering leader, develop your personal philosophy, your set of guiding principles. Know your values, or you will be inclined to compromise. Compromising details or method matters little. Compromising essential values leads to defeat.

In developing your guiding principles, realize that a "good hand" or a "good head" is not what your team needs. You need head, hand, and heart. Though we are limited in our physical and mental capabilities, our hearts are infinite in their capacity to energetically commit. When the heart is engaged, we more fully utilize our physical and mental capabilities. An empowering leader enlists the full person and secures holistic engagement, thus maximizing performance.

———

In this powerful portion of Ronald Reagan's farewell speech, given January 11, 1989, he stated the truth about empowering ideals:

"...I won a nickname, 'The Great Communicator.' But I never thought it was my style or the words I used that made a difference....I wasn't a great communicator, but I communicated great things, and they didn't spring full bloom from my brow, they came from the heart of a great nation—from our experience, our wisdom, and our belief in the principles that have guided us for two centuries.

They called it the Reagan revolution. Well, I'll accept that, but for me it always seemed more like the great rediscovery, a rediscovery of our values and our common sense."[21]

Not long after Reagan's speech at the Brandenburg Gate, when he challenged Gorbachev to "tear down this wall," "the wall did come tumbling down, and Reagan's prophecies all came true."[22] Reagan did not just predict that this would occur; he actively worked to make his vision a reality. He resisted the temptation to accept the status quo, though many thought what he advocated could not be done. Challenge your own team to tear down the walls impeding progress in your organization. Leading from your high ideals can make it so.

As an empowering leader, *you* make it happen by constantly referring to the ultimate values of your organization. Your words inspire your team to use their creative ingenuity to achieve seemingly impossible goals. By inspiring your team and referring to your mission, vision, and values, saying something and believing it really does make it so.

Leadership Principle 2

"Your Cadette troop 1541 sounds like a real active group with some achievements to be proud of. I wish you well on your plans for a trip to Europe. I've enclosed a small contribution for your fundraising campaign. After all [we] presidents have to stick together."

Ronald Reagan, letter to the 13-yr.-old president
of a Girl Scout troop[1]

Become Genuinely Interested ~ Show Compassionate Empathy

During the Vietnam War, Governor Reagan received a letter from a soldier overseas. The soldier told Reagan he would be in Vietnam for his wedding anniversary, and he was concerned that the card he sent might not reach his wife in Orangevale. He asked if the governor would please call her and tell her how much her husband loved her.

Reagan didn't call. Instead, without telling his staff where he was going, he left the office a little early on the anniversary day and personally delivered a dozen red roses to the wife on behalf of her husband. He then spent

41

over an hour chatting with her about the couple's children.[2] If Reagan had simply done what the soldier had asked, it would have been a special favor. His taking time to visit a stranger was an extraordinary manifestation of his genuine interest in others.

A genuine liking for and a sincere interest in others naturally results in personal charisma and magnetism. By developing the habit of caring for and about others, you become a dynamic, empowering leader. By taking a personal interest in the people you work with, you strengthen your ability to lead. Only when you have shown genuine interest in others can you expect them to take an interest in you.

Empathy enables us to use our heads as well as our hearts in our relations with others. Empathy is similar to sympathy; but whereas sympathy says, "I feel as you do," empathy says, "I know how you feel." By developing the ability to appreciate the feelings of others without becoming too emotionally involved, we can communicate our sincere interest. We can then reach a meeting of minds, and others will be motivated to accept our communications and act on them.

———

In the early 1930s, when Reagan was a

college football player, racial prejudice was common. One time the Eureka College football team passed through Reagan's hometown of Dixon, Illinois and planned to spend the night there. Since he knew the town, Reagan accompanied the coach into the local hotel to book rooms for the team. When the hotel refused to accommodate the black team members, the coach angrily decided the whole team would sleep on the bus.

Reagan thought inconveniencing the whole team would just make the black teammates feel worse. Instead, Reagan told the coach he would say that the hotel did not have room for everyone and invite the black players to stay with him at his parents' house. The coach asked Reagan if he was sure he did not need to check it out with his parents first. Reagan said he didn't need to. He knew his parents would welcome his teammates.

Mrs. Nelle Reagan "was absolutely color blind when it came to racial matters; these fellows were just two of my friends," Reagan later wrote.[3] Taking personal interest in the needs of others came naturally to Reagan. He had been raised to look out for and care about other people.

Thankfully, explicit racial prejudice is not as common today as it used to be; but there are other less obvious forms of prejudice. Often, the tendency to prejudge others is less about race or gender than about position and title. Some managers tend to be prejudiced against the ideas and views of those in other departments: the prejudice of engineering toward sales, sales toward finance, operations toward engineering, contractors toward architects, etc. The empowering leader sets aside any and all inclinations to prejudge and instead weighs each idea on its merits.

———

Ronald Reagan was in tune with others, no matter who they were. He cultivated a genuine interest in them. "It didn't matter who you were or what your position in life was," said Reagan advisor and deputy chief of staff Mike Deaver. "Ronald Reagan treated everybody the same. Whether you were a soldier's wife or the Queen of England, you got the same treatment from Ronald Reagan. I was with him in Windsor Castle, and I can testify that Reagan treated Queen Elizabeth exactly the same way he treated White House stewards—with grace, kindness, and respect."[4] He did not let success distance him from those on the rungs below him. Through his positions of leadership, Reagan actively took an interest in others and in their concerns and needs.

When young Ronald Reagan first came to Hollywood in the early 1940s, he grudgingly joined the actors' union, the Screen Actors Guild. He did not know why a union was necessary but soon learned from older actors that before the SAG, they often had been exploited by the studios. While major stars could negotiate their contracts and working conditions, young contract players could not.[5]

Reagan joined the SAG board of directors to represent young contract players. When he attended his first directors' meeting, he expected to see people like himself, "lesser actors" who could be exploited by the studios. In fact, he met some of Hollywood's top stars, including Cary Grant and James Cagney.[6]

In his autobiography, Reagan wrote of those who ran the union: "Most were big box-office draws who could easily command huge salaries and didn't need the Guild's help to negotiate their wages. But they enthusiastically gave their time and prestige to assure that lesser players like me got a fair shake. That night I told myself that if I ever became a star, I'd do as much as I could to help the actors and actresses at the bottom of the ladder."[7]

Reagan eventually served seven effective terms as president of the Screen Actors Guild. He stood up to Communist-front organizations in order to protect the freedom of artists in

Hollywood to use their creativity without the control of those who wanted to use the arts for propaganda. He proved himself a tough negotiator between actors and studios. He became identified so much with the union that his acting career waned: Directors thought of him as Reagan the negotiator rather than Reagan the actor.[8] While Reagan sacrificed his acting career in the interest of others in his profession, the door to wider public service opened.

Empowering leaders give back. They take part in their industry associations and community organizations. They are willing to help others succeed, even if getting involved might require sacrifices in their own careers. They give freely without expecting return and often end up getting far more than they gave. Through networking in their communities, they gain access and influence. Through their association, involvement, and working with volunteers, they strengthen their leadership skills and ability to engage and motivate their own teams.

———

Leaders are readers, life-long learners who cultivate an interest in a broad range of subjects, not just their own businesses or areas of specialty. They take an interest in the affairs of others. Reagan always had an inquisitive mind and loved to learn new things. "He wouldn't feel right without having something to read," his son Ron Reagan told Peter Robinson, "so he'd always have a book going."[9] He read widely, which meant that he was not confined to talking about only a few things. Sometimes he would surprise people by his interest in and knowledge of their own subject of expertise.

Ed Meese met Reagan for the first time when Reagan had just become governor of California. Meese recalled that they discussed "law enforcement and crime control, the things I had spent the last ten years working on." He was surprised to find Reagan so well-informed in the very areas in which Meese was an expert. He was so impressed with Reagan's interest in a wide range of subjects that he agreed on the spot to become his new chief of staff.[10]

Reagan did not make a big deal out of his own knowledge. His goal in reading was to understand other people and their ideas better. During the White House years, his press secretary Marlin Fitzwater wanted to counter the press's opinion that the president was an "amiable dunce" by releasing a list of the stack of books Reagan had brought on a trip to Europe. Reagan replied that "it didn't really matter to him, but it was probably unnecessary."[11] Reagan was not out to impress anyone, and Fitzwater did not mention the books to the reporters.

———

Empowering leaders never lose touch with their roots and relate to the interests, fears, and concerns of everyone on their team. Reagan's talent was to show his interest in the concerns of Americans by speaking as one of them. He could do this because he *was* one of them. Reagan succeeded as a communicator because he wrote "for the ear." His speeches were meant to be listened to. He successfully communicated his interest in others through his careful attention to his speeches.

Helen Thomas, dean of the White House press corps, praised Reagan's ability to connect with Americans: "[W]hen it came to talking to people, there was no one who could compare to him. His stable of speechwriters came up with the draft, but Reagan came up with the delivery. He would rewrite a speech in a way that connected with every American, and practiced every pause and the cadence until he had it down with his own perfect timing."[12]

Your opportunities to speak before audiences may never compare with presidential addresses to the nation. However, if you are wise you will recognize that these opportunities are times for which you should prepare, whether they are teleconferences, team meetings you are leading, or staff meetings in which you are giving a report. On any of these occasions you are making an impression that goes deeper than the normal daily impression of one-on-one encounters. Through proper preparation you can have significant influence on the direction of events and propel your own career forward.

———

Reagan never lost touch with the small-town America in which he grew up. He knew what it was like to struggle financially. He was one of the minority to get a college education in those days, but he still found himself one of millions of Americans out of work during the Depression. The son of an alcoholic father and a heroically forgiving mother, he personally empathized with the down-and-out. A movie actor, he understood celebrity and wealth. A divorcé who later married the love of his life, Nancy, he knew that money, fame, and popularity are not the sources of happiness.

The ups and downs of his journey from Dixon to D.C. went into making Reagan who he was: an American grateful for what an ordinary person can accomplish in this country. Success did not make him elitist; it made him proud to be an American. He treated people as if they were all members of his family, the American family.

Promotion or a quick flight to a higher position can easily cause some to become "puffed up," haughty, out of touch, and arrogant. If you allow this to happen, it is only a matter of time before you lose your edge as a leader. Unless you remember who you are and where you came from and approach your role with humility, your advancement will come to a halt, and you are likely to end up back where you started.

———

Reagan used letter writing to show his interest in others. During his presidency, it was one of the few ways he could interact directly with ordinary Americans. A president receives hundreds of thousands of letters, more than anyone could ever read or respond to. Reagan liked to read and answer as many as he could, making time every week to read and answer at least fifty letters. Some members of his staff thought this was a waste of the president's time, but Reagan was genuinely interested in what Americans had to say.[13]

Reagan showed a personal interest in the individuals he wrote to, addressing those he had never met personally as if they were his friends and relatives. He was never artificial, though; and he did not talk down to anyone, as public figures sometimes do when trying to "be ordinary people." He was unfailingly courteous, often apologizing for the time it took him to respond to letters, even when the turn-around time was only a few weeks.

Reagan did not just thank the writer and say something formulaic about his administration and his commitment to the American people. He took the time to respond to their comments, concerns, and criticisms. He expressed personal concern for their specific struggles. He told stories from his own life. He reminisced with older Americans; he gave friendly advice to the young. He wished them well and occasionally invited them to write again and direct their letters through his personal secretary.

If Reagan was particularly touched by someone's story—a family who had adopted several handicapped children, for example—he would even send a personal check to help out. Sometimes people wanted to keep the checks as souvenirs, and he would tell them to cash the check and his accountant would return it to them.[14] Other times banks did not want to cash the checks because the presidential signature was worth more than the amount![15]

It is challenging for most of us to read and respond to all the e-mail we receive every day, but empowering leaders find ways to make the time. Many top executives keep in touch through the discipline of reading every customer comment card and responding as appropriate. Empowering leaders take the time to write notes: personal notes, notes on paychecks, notes of encouragement, birthday cards, notes on newspaper articles, notes on reports. Develop the habit of writing at least six notes a day. You will increase the morale of your team and enhance your two-way communication with them.

———

Reagan impressed others by the way he treated each person he met as a unique and important individual. He made time for them, even if they were not "important people." For Reagan, there were no "important people." There were just people, and each was special.

During the 1970s, Reagan recorded radio commentaries in a studio in California. Many years later, his producer Harry O'Connor recalled that Reagan was asked on an occasion to sign a birthday card for one of the receptionists. Reagan took it to her himself and then volunteered to sing "Happy Birthday" to her.[16]

Fred Ryan, Reagan's chief of staff after he left the presidency, remembered a time Reagan had just finished giving a speech in Arizona to two thousand people. Reagan was worried about getting to Los Angeles in time to meet with a young Boy Scout scheduled to see him as soon as he got back. He did not want to miss the appointment.[17]

Reagan had a policy during his retirement that anyone who had ever worked for him could call on him at his Los Angeles office. Many came to see him who had worked in departments below him but had never actually met him.[18]

Kathy Osborne, Reagan's personal secretary in Sacramento and in Washington, attested that Reagan would put aside whatever he was working on, no matter how serious, and give his full attention to individuals receiving special honors in the Oval Office. He would "treat the visitor as if he or she were the most important person in the world," she said.[19]

"...Reagan seemed to relate to everyone, regardless of their position in life...," wrote his senior foreign affairs advisor Dinesh D'Souza. "He would engage in good-natured banter with the governor of a large state, and a few minutes later would have an equally amiable exchange with a hotel doorman or one of his Secret Service agents....Reagan seemed to have a special affection for the unfashionable folk—the cops and nuns and refuseniks and Sons of Italy. However incongruous they seemed in corridors lined with dapper professionals, all these people could be seen around the White House during the Reagan years."[20]

Empowering leaders in every walk of life take a genuine interest in others. Wall Street analysts and mutual fund managers have begun factoring in employee morale when calculating future stock values. In terms of morale, Ronald Reagan was a success. When he left the presidency in 1989, he was the most popular outgoing president since Eisenhower.[21] Ed Meese gave the credit to Reagan's genuine interest in others: "The concerns and aspirations of the average citizen were the touchstones of his career in government and accounted for much of his success."[22] Throughout his career in public office Reagan displayed this interest in people and their lives.

———

Speechwriter Peter Robinson told a story which further illustrates this. Late one evening he and Chase Untermeyer, an advisor to Vice President Bush, were busy rewriting a speech. They were having a rough time, semi-conscious of a vacuum cleaner making noise in the hall outside and imagining themselves to be alone with the West Wing janitors. Suddenly, the president stuck his head in the door, "grinned, waved, and gave us a wink."

"That little encounter with the President won't show up in any history book," wrote Robinson. "It didn't even make for much of a story when I telephoned my parents that night....But twenty years later, I can still replay the encounter in my mind as if in slow motion....Afterward, Chase and I felt better. We felt refreshed....

"'How,' I asked, turning to Chase, 'did such a nice guy ever get to be President?'"[23]

Managing by wandering around is not something that empowering leaders have to be forced to do. They do it instinctively because they care and are genuinely interested. They want to know how people are doing, what is really going on, and how things are working out. Of course, as a manager you have many demands on your time; you have a job to do. If you can develop the discipline of stopping for a moment and giving undivided attention to those who seek it, to those you encounter, you may be amazed at the difference it can make in your, their, and your company's life.

———

When giving a speech at a dinner, Reagan felt unconnected if he ate alone in his hotel room and then came in at the end for the speech. He preferred to eat with the people to whom he would be speaking. He used the time to get in touch with those in the room, to learn their interests, issues, and concerns. Every group was different, composed of different individuals.

"Between bites, Reagan would express a deep interest in whatever occasion had brought the group together," said Mike Deaver. "He was always listening and learning."[24] He never "worked a room." He paid attention to the individual with whom he was talking. "He would never peek over his conversation partner's shoulder. Big or small, important or just an Average Joe or Jane, this person became the subject of his interest, and the rest of the room was a blur."[25]

It may only take a brief moment of acknowledgment to make someone's day. If you are looking for a prescriptive technique for becoming genuinely interested in others, you may come up short-handed. Genuine interest is more about who you are than what you do. It is about getting your mind off yourself. Move past the natural inclination to think of your schedule, your needs, and "what's in it for me."

As you develop and practice this character trait of true caring and compassion, you will increase your influence with others and become an empowering leader. Compassion provides the personal strength required for true empathy. We must have empathy before we can, with sincerity, employ the remaining 13 Leadership Principles.

Leadership Principle 3

"I'm not worried about the deficit: it's big enough to take care of itself."

Ronald Reagan[1]

Don't Criticize, Condemn, or Complain

In the late 1960s and early 1970s student protests, antiwar protests, and cultural changes made Ronald Reagan's two terms as governor of California particularly challenging. He endured assassination plots and attempted fire-bombings of his family's residence. In such a climate, strong words are expected and often required.

While Reagan was no push-over, he tried to elevate disputes to a civilized level of conversation. In *Reagan's War*, Peter Schweizer recorded that when Black Panther leader Eldridge Cleaver led five thousand students in shouting profanity, Reagan replied that "he was glad to have a dialogue with his critics, but not the four-letter-word kind."[2]

It is easy to succumb to the temptation to descend to the lowest common denominator.

58

When leaders lose their temper, they lose the respect of others. When you lose the respect of others, you lose your opportunity to lead. The empowering leader chooses to raise the bar rather than lower it. Reagan chose to keep the bar high, and in doing so he won the respect of others.

In working with people with whom we disagree or whose performance is less than perfect, our natural tendency is to criticize, condemn, and complain. These are the easiest ways to handle upset, irritation, dissatisfaction, and disagreement. While easy to employ, these seldom achieve positive results.

Here are three C's you can use to replace criticizing, condemning, and complaining: concern, coaching, and correcting. Concern is easy to distinguish from criticizing, condemning, and complaining. Concern is showing a sincere interest in helping others improve their performance and approaching them in a way that shows your first interest is their success.

Coaching is used to improve a person's performance when they are not violating a standard and there is room for improvement in their performance and effectiveness. People listen when you are complimentary and feel it is possible that you can assist them. Coaching requires you as an empowering leader to sharpen your own observation skills.

An empowering leader coaches others by first pointing out what they are doing that is satisfactory, appropriate, and effective. This compliment is followed by a specific change they can make to improve their performance, prefaced by: "I have a suggestion that might help you improve; may I mention it?" or "I have an idea that could make it a little easier, safer, faster, etc." After providing the specific behavior-oriented way to improve performance, follow your suggestion with a statement of belief in them. Predict the success and practical outcome of the change. Provide encouragement, such as: "You are going to be really good at this" or "You are going to be one of our best."

Use correction when someone is clearly violating a standard: not being at work on time, failing to wear safety equipment, approaching a customer in an inappropriate manner, failing to lock out/tag out, inappropriate interaction with an associate or in a meeting. Correction can begin by stating the observed behavior: "Bill, I noticed you were late. What happened?" Listen actively and attentively to their response. When you reply, restate the standard we must live up to and the reason for its importance. Then describe the desired positive change in performance you want to see: "The next time...." Get an agreement: "Can I count on you?" It is important to end on a positive note: "I'm sure you will...."

Concern, coaching, and correcting are positive, empowering ways to improve performance that is only made worse by criticizing, condemning, and complaining. These three positive C's minimize your team's fear of criticism and failure, reinforce understanding, build skills, facilitate growth in their jobs, and help everyone on the path toward excellence. As progress is made, be sure to give praise and encouragement. Focus on your team's accomplishments.

———

Dinesh D'Souza, Reagan's senior foreign affairs advisor, said that President Reagan preferred to speak to what was good in people rather than to be a negative critic. "Like Lincoln," D'Souza wrote, "Reagan saw the depth of human frailty but appealed to the better angels of our nature. He spoke of achievement rather than indolence, triumph instead of failure, goodness instead of depravity....But he was also a pragmatist: he knew that most people respond better to encouragement than to harsh criticism."[3]

Criticism is pointing out what you do not like about someone or their performance in a way that is taken personally. This inclination is so common that management texts have developed and popularized the idea of "constructive criticism." The only problem with this idea is that criticism by its nature is taken personally. When people feel under attack, they become defensive. It is hard to imagine how the result can be constructive. Even if you get the behavior change you want, leaving others wounded can hardly be called leadership.

———

Part of not criticizing is cultivating a positive attitude. When Peggy Noonan was a new speechwriter for President Reagan, another writer advised her, "And remember, it always has to be positive with him. Never [write], 'I'll never forget,' always 'I'll always remember.'"[4]

White House press aide Larry Speakes remembered that Reagan made a conscious effort to be gracious at the 1986 dedication of the Carter Presidential Library, putting the acrimony of the 1980 campaign behind him. "We have made up our minds that no matter what happens, we're going to be gracious," Reagan told Speakes.

In his speech, Reagan painted a positive image of Carter, remembering him in the Oval Office "with an air of intense concentration," working to free the hostages in Iran and to find a way to peace in the Middle East. Carter was touched by Reagan's graciousness, commenting, "I think I now understand more clearly than I ever had before why you won in November 1980, and I lost."[5]

One of the first recommendations for being an empowering leader is to develop the ability to withhold judgment. Instead, find a positive means of bringing others to examine their own actions or positions. Empowering leaders exercise the creativity required to find and keep the high ground, to make a point without resorting to cutting, critical character assassination. They develop the ability to correct a course of action, bring team members back into alignment, or point out what is not working without resorting to criticism.

———

Nothing is more powerful than humor in dealing positively with criticism—both when receiving criticism and when making necessary points to opponents and to team members. Criticism cuts off communication and productivity and breeds resentment in their place.

During the 1976 presidential campaign Reagan joked: "The government in Washington is spending some $7 million every minute I talk to you. There's no connection between my talking and their spending, and if they'll stop spending, I'll stop talking."[6]

During his presidency, Reagan struggled to reduce the federal deficit and domestic spending. Occasionally, wrote Dinesh D'Souza, "[Reagan's] frustration would give way to grim jokes. At a cabinet meeting he was informed that as part of congressional subsidies to the dairy industry, the federal government was stabilizing market prices by buying from producers, with the result that government warehouses currently had 478 million pounds of surplus butter. 'Four hundred and seventy eight million pounds of butter!' Reagan gasped. 'Does anyone know where we can find four hundred and seventy eight million pounds of popcorn?'"[7]

Ronald Reagan had both the creativity and the wit to deflect the criticism of others, to be gracious in the face of annoyance, and to make his points without stooping to cheap shots or character assassination. Along with not taking himself too seriously, he effectively used his wit to avoid bluntly putting others down. Whereas humor takes a quick wit, criticism requires neither creativity nor wit.

———

In politics, as in business, it is necessary to point out the differences between yourself and your competitors. Humor is a great way to do this without being mean-spirited or putting people down. Causing laughter breaks the tension and effectively deflects the criticism of others.

When speaking of his California gubernatorial opponent, Pat Brown, Reagan said, "The governor talks about *his* lakes and *his* reservoirs; you have the feeling that when he leaves office he'll take them with him."[8]

On truth in government, he said: "The credibility gap is so great in Washington they told us the truth the other day hoping we wouldn't believe it."[9]

At a banquet at which Reagan introduced comedian Bob Hope, President Reagan noted that Hope "has two great loves. He loves to entertain and he loves golf. Just the other day he asked me, 'What's your handicap?' And I said, 'Congress.'"[10]

During the 1981 budget debate, Illinois Governor James Thompson "warned the President that some of his colleagues would accept Reagan's budget cuts over their dead bodies, [and] Reagan quipped, 'Well, maybe over their dead bodies isn't a bad idea.'"[11]

Reagan's wit and humor are legendary. Family friend Jean Smith said that Reagan's jokes softened the positions with which he disagreed. He would make others laugh.[12]

While Reagan differentiated himself from his opponents, editor and commentator M. Stanton Evans has noted that ad hominem attacks were completely out of character for him.[13]

"He gave as good as he got," wrote journalist and Reagan biographer Lou Cannon, "but he was never vicious about an opponent. He was not out to destroy anyone. He might vehemently attack someone's policy or proposal, but not the person."[14]

The easiest thing to do in politics, and the thing everyone says they hate about politics, is "negative campaigning." It is a lot easier to respond to an opponent's attacks with negative criticism than to find a way to keep the debate civil, focused, and constructive. Stay positive, focus on the issues at hand, and find a way to soften necessary points of disagreement. Get in step before you disagree about anything; find the point of agreement. "I know you want to make the right decision," "I used to feel the same way until I found out...," and "That's a good question" are good starting points.

———

When President Reagan visited China, the

Communist government edited his address. The American press corps asked him what he thought of the government preventing his message from getting through to the Chinese people. "Reagan just smiled at all of us," wrote Helen Thomas, "and replied, 'Oh, it didn't bother me at all. You guys do it all the time.'"[15]

The press loves to bait public figures. Reagan had the wit and the restraint not to hit back. When the press attacked him early in his first term as governor, Reagan quipped, "I had been led to believe there was a honeymoon period, but evidently I lost the license on the way to church."[16]

Throughout his presidency Reagan maintained a cordial relationship with the press. Helen Thomas said, "For all the pointed questions I lobbed at Reagan in his eight years in office, he never seemed to take any personal umbrage, and I think that was true of his attitude toward all the reporters."[17]

Sam Donaldson commented that Reagan was "secure enough" about himself that he could let criticism from the press and others "[roll] off his back more than I've seen it roll off other Presidents' backs."[18]

Your confidence as an empowering leader comes from believing in the mission, vision, and values which are at the center of who you are and of what you do as an organization. When you believe in your principles, you do not have to be defensive when they—or you—are criticized. You will not need to stoop to petty behavior, back stabbing, or skulduggery. Instead, you will find the confidence, serenity, and personal security that kept Reagan strong in the face of criticism.

———

As president, Reagan refused to take the easy road of condemnation and blame. Ed Meese recalled that during the beginning of Reagan's administration, the president "was under obvious pressure to 'bash' the Fed and seek easy money. But he steadfastly refused. On the contrary, he often conveyed to Fed Chairman Paul Volcker...that the administration stood by the Fed in following a path of prudent money growth, even though the President himself was under great criticism because of the recession. Again, a case of decisive leadership and political courage—though one seldom publicized."[19]

Reagan wouldn't "bash the Fed," nor would he attack his team members publicly or privately. "While he never tried to be 'buddies' with those who worked for him," said Meese, "he was always friendly and genial...."[20]

Condemning is when we criticize

someone behind their back instead of confronting them directly. This could be an attempt to solve problems or to seek advice from a third party. Sometimes it springs from feelings of frustration. More often, it is just a lack of the courage required to go direct. Whatever the reason, condemnation is always destructive of trust and morale. It is so tempting to deflect or shift responsibility, to blame others, and to try to make excuses for failed performance: "It's the home office's (or another department's) fault," "It's poor engineering," or "That's our supplier's fault."

When we fall into a habit of condemning, we create a triangular scenario within the organization. We go to a third party and tell what we do not like about the first party. The third party goes to the first party (even though we may have pledged them to confidentiality), and round and round it goes. We earn a reputation for being untrustworthy and disloyal. Credibility, trust, respect, opportunities for real communication, and all hope of teamwork are lost.

Tempers can flare when we do not address the reality of a situation—what is not working or what needs to be changed. When things are not working or someone's behavior needs to change, it is crucial that we have the courage to go direct, to speak to those involved—not to talk behind their backs. Take stock of what is going on: Accumulate data on how often the machine broke down, etc. In these situations, it helps to remember that we do not build ourselves up by making others look bad. Apply Reagan's "eleventh commandment," "Thou shalt not speak ill of a fellow Republican," to your team, too.

———

On a visit to Vanderbilt University as governor of California, Reagan was confronted by a young heckler. "Hey Ronnie," the heckler yelled, "what do you think of pot?...Your generation needed your martinis, right, Ronnie?"

"You're right, we did need our martinis, but I can still hope that a generation would come along that wouldn't *need* anything."[21]

Reagan chose to counsel rather than to condemn. He did not accept the justification of negative behavior by other negative behavior. Instead, he referred back to the ideal, believing that we can challenge ourselves to rise above the least common denominator.

———

In a letter to a teenager named Scott Osborne, Reagan tactfully commented on the young man's interest in alcohol:

"Scott, I shouldn't do this, but I have to argue with you a bit on your postscript about age 18 and the right to drink....Now don't think I'm a hypocrite....I also recall feeling exactly as you do now....At that age (about 18) getting drunk seemed like the thing to do....Then, before something too awful happened (although there were a few near scrapes) I realized that I was abusing the machinery, this body. We only get one you know....

"Forgive me for playing grandpa—but think about it a little. Become an architect or, if you change your mind—whatever, and we'll celebrate your graduation with a champagne toast, and I'll furnish the wine."[22]

Reagan chose to be gracious and positive when offering advice to those who wrote to him. He refused to condemn. He chose to counsel instead. He did not raise himself up at the expense of others.

"Imagine a man nobody hates...," wrote Peggy Noonan. "[Reagan] was never dark, never mean, never waited for the sound of the door closing to say, 'What a fool,' didn't seethe, had no malice. People could tell he trusted their motives. It brought out the best in the best of them, who acted better for the compliment...."[23]

In your role as a leader, you will be given many opportunities to counsel, by refraining from moralizing while holding the high ground. You will build rapport, earn respect, and through the process help team members reexamine their approach and behavior. You are in a unique position to bring the best out of them and touch their lives in a way that can change them forever.

———

"Because Ronnie really believes what his mother taught him, that everything happens for a purpose, he doesn't let setbacks or disappointments get him down," wrote Nancy Reagan in her memoir, *My Turn*. Reagan wrote a poem in high school that began:

"I wonder what it's all about, and why
We suffer so, when little things
          go wrong?
We make our life a struggle,
When life should be a song."

"This attitude is why," Nancy continued, "in my next life, I'd like to come back as Ronald Reagan."[24]

Complaining is finding fault, pointing out what is wrong versus what is right. It focuses on the flaw, the speck, versus the abundance of virtue. In a climate of criticizing and condemning, you find a lot of complaining.

Nancy Reagan has often said that her husband was not a complainer. "I've almost never heard him complain," she wrote. "If something is bothering Ronnie, he'll rarely mention it."[25]

Former Canadian Prime Minister Brian Mulroney said of Reagan: "He always conducted himself with a great amount of courtesy. I never saw him be rude to anyone, though some were rude to him. I never saw him react in anger at a high-level meeting, nor did he throw his weight around. He always spoke softly....He knew how the American people wanted a president to conduct himself, and that is exactly what he did."[26]

If you aspire to be an empowering leader who can win the hearts of your team, do as Ronald Reagan did. Deny the natural inclination to criticize, condemn, and complain. Resist the temptation to think, "I criticize, therefore I am." Develop your sense of humor and the ability either to courageously go direct or to withhold judgment entirely. Adopt an optimistic frame of mind which eliminates the need to complain. As you do, you will go a long way toward winning the respect, admiration, cooperation, and enthusiastic support of those around you.

Leadership Principle 4

"I couldn't help but think that if the people of the world judged Americans by what they saw of you, then they would think, 'Americans? Well, they're generous and full of serious effort; they're full of high spirits; they're motivated by all the best things. They're truly a nation of champions."

Ronald Reagan, during the 1984 Olympics in Los Angeles[1]

Provide Acknowledgment

Helen Thomas, dean of the White House Press Corps, has covered every president since John F. Kennedy. When she received the National Press Club's Fourth Estate Award in 1984, Reagan wrote her a friendly and complimentary letter in which he said: "You have a worldwide reputation for being the best—always first, always accurate, always fair....[Y]ou are an inspiration to all who seek to be good reporters....You are not only a fine and respected professional; you have also become an important part of the American Presidency. I am proud to salute you tonight."[2] In the White House, Ronald Reagan made a habit of giving compliments even to those who often assumed an adversarial posture toward him.

Acknowledgment wins friends and builds your team. When an empowering leader publicly expresses gratitude or recognizes achievement, it encourages others to do the same. Providing acknowledgment builds morale in a team, organization, or (in Ronald Reagan's case) the nation. Ronald Reagan acknowledged the strengths of those with whom he worked.

Empowering leaders recognize that in every situation, regardless of their position, their job is to create an atmosphere that builds people. We all tend to take others for granted. Leaders bring out the best in others and make them successful by helping them see their own potential. They empower others to aim higher, to achieve greater things, and to believe even more in themselves. They carefully pay positive attention and give effective approval, appreciation, and praise to everyone around them.

———

In a 1942 interview with *Photoplay*, a fan magazine, Ronald Reagan had the humility to say of himself, "...I'm not [Errol] Flynn or [Charles] Boyer, and well I know it."[3] When Reagan later entered political life, his opponents loved to call him a "B" actor, even though an early 1940s poll showed him to be as popular with audiences as Laurence Olivier.[4] Reagan could have responded defensively, complained, or retaliated. He did not, because he had cultivated the habit of graciously acknowledging the talents of others.

Rather than being bitter about not being at the top, Reagan preferred to take pride in the fact that he played his roles as well as he could. And most importantly, he used opportunities to talk about his own career to acknowledge the talent and success of his "A" colleagues. He told *Photoplay*:

"Thanks to some good advice from... [actor] Pat O'Brien, I played those 'B's' as if they were 'A's.' You see, the boss only goes by results. If I do a part carelessly because I doubt its importance, no one is going to write a subtitle explaining that Ronald Reagan didn't feel the part was important, therefore he didn't give it very much....

"Quite a few times, before *Knute Rockne* [his big break], parts came up in pictures that I thought I'd like to play. In *Dark Victory* with Bette Davis, for example, they handed me a bit part. I stewed around a bit, wishing I'd got the part [Humphrey] Bogart played in that picture. Then I realized I couldn't top Bogey in that. It was his dish, not mine. In *Kings Row*, Parris was not for me, but Drake, I think, was. In *Desperate Journey*, Flynn's spot is his, not mine.

"But I knew I could deliver the Gipp...."[5]

Empowering leaders acknowledge the accomplishments of others and praise their talents, skills, and achievements. They are not threatened by others' achievements, even if their promotion was one they had hoped to receive themselves. On the contrary, they rejoice in their teammates' success, focusing on who really is best suited to the job, the expanded role, or the promotion. They are generous in acknowledging the greatness of others. You will be "passed over" at least once or twice in your career. Graciousness will go a long way toward positioning you for the next opportunity, which may come sooner than you think.

———

Ronald Reagan had a habit of complimenting people whenever possible, directly or indirectly, even in the midst of serious philosophical or policy differences. He was generous in acknowledging the positive steps taken by other world leaders and gave them credit for the incredible changes that swept the world under their leadership.

President Reagan had a special relationship with British Prime Minister

Margaret Thatcher. She was such a close political ally that he described her as "the other woman in my life."[6] While they generally agreed in their foreign policy, they did have a few differences.

On one such occasion, the prime minister called to vehemently express her displeasure with Reagan's position. "Reagan took the telephone away from his ear, placed his hand over the speaker, and said to his aides, 'Isn't she *marvelous?*'"[7] He did not react defensively to her input; he appreciated her confidence in speaking to him honestly. He praised her strength to others.

During the Westland affair, a period of controversy for the prime minister, Reagan called Thatcher to express his support and reaffirm his friendship. She deeply appreciated his acknowledgment, writing in *The Downing Street Years*: "...I also had staunch friends who rallied round. Not the least of these was President Reagan who telephoned me...at No. 10. He said that he was furious that anyone had the gall to challenge my integrity. He wanted me to know that 'out here in the colonies' I had a friend. He urged me to go out 'and do my darndest'. I appreciated his call."[8]

We all can think of a time when outside adversaries have tried to "find daylight" between us and our fellow teammates, hoping to exploit difficult situations or minor disagreements to sow discord within the team. When this happened during the Reagan administration, the president was loyal to his cabinet, encouraging members under attack.

———

William Bennett had been secretary of education for only a few weeks when he came under an intense media attack. He was trying to implement the president's ideals by bringing more responsibility into the educational system, and he quickly became a controversial figure. At a cabinet meeting, President Reagan came to the last item on the agenda, a folder labeled "Bennett."

"I was pretty isolated at this point," Bennett recalled, "and the president started to read aloud just the [newspaper] headlines. 'BENNETT, A DUNCE IN THE CLASSROOM,'...'BENNETT MUST BE FIRED.'

"...I was sinking farther and farther in my seat....Reagan put the last clipping in and...said, 'Now, that's Bill Bennett's first three weeks in office. What's wrong with the rest of you?'

"It was...one of the kindest and most considerate things anybody ever did for me....[I]t taught me what a leader can do, and what it can mean to the morale of people to have done that."

When Bennett thanked the president for taking up for him publicly, Reagan replied, "You know, they like to criticize me for being in show business. But one thing you learn...[is] there's a difference between the critics and the box office. Don't worry about the critics, just keep doing your job."[9]

Effective praise changes the way the receivers view themselves. Watch your employees. Think back to when someone demonstrated a praiseworthy trait. Put that trait into a word (determination, creativity, initiative...), and tell that person what you think of them. Let others know how their individual performance specifically contributes to the successful fulfillment of the organization's mission; directly link what each person does to the delivery of your service or product. Solicit everyone's partnership in the establishment of a culture in which the entire team is expressly appreciated and recognized for the work they do.

When people are struggling and feel they have two strikes against them, empowering leaders do not wait for the home run to provide encouragement, support, and praise. They take the opportunity to offer encouragement which provides others with the courage to try again, to put out the extra effort needed to win. A bad quarter, an accident, failing to hit key targets, or losing a key team member are times when such encouragement is needed most to ensure the team does not lose heart.

Empowering leaders do not let fear and hesitation get in the way of offering all three kinds of acknowledgment: a direct compliment, an indirect compliment (telling a third party about someone), and a third-party compliment (telling someone the good things others have said about them). When it is impossible to express appreciation or thanks directly, or the moment has passed you by, an indirect compliment is the next best thing.

The most powerful compliment of all may be the third-party compliment because your sincerity cannot be questioned. You are quoting another person, and yet you must agree or you would not pass on the compliment. When you acknowledge others' good qualities and contributions, you immeasurably increase the effectiveness of the total effort.

———

Reagan did not take sole credit for the massive achievements both in this country and in the cause of world peace and freedom which resulted largely from his presidency. Instead, he shared the credit with others. Ed Meese wrote that "the most complete overview of the Reagan years is the President's own memoir, *An American Life*." However, Meese added that "[e]ven this memoir is limited...in one essential aspect: the President likes neither to claim credit for himself nor to apportion blame to others. He is thus reluctant to stake a claim for himself in history."[10] Reagan preferred to point to the greatness of others.

During his presidency Reagan challenged Mikhail Gorbachev to join him in changing the relationship between their countries. In *An American Life*, Reagan positively acknowledged Gorbachev as "an intelligent man and a good listener."[11] At the 1990 dedication of the Westminster College Cold War Memorial in Fulton, Missouri, Reagan praised Gorbachev:

"A new Soviet leader appeared on the scene, untainted by the past, unwilling to be shackled by crumbling orthodoxies. With the rise of Mikhail Gorbachev came the end of numbing oppression. Glasnost introduced openness to the world's most closed society. Perestroika held out the promise of a better life, achieved through democratic institutions and a market economy. And real arms control came to pass, as an entire class of weapons was eliminated for the first time in the atomic age."[12]

He also credited his other allies: "I was by

no means alone. Principled leaders like Helmut Kohl and Margaret Thatcher reinforced our message that the West would not be blackmailed and that the only rational course was to return to the bargaining table in Geneva and work out real and lasting arms reductions fair to both sides."[13]

Reagan always insisted that credit be given where credit was due. He knew that President Carter worked until the moment of leaving office to get the American hostages freed in Iran. Reagan believed the Iranian government was continuing to hold the hostages past the hour of his inauguration merely to spite Carter. Reagan insisted that should the hostages be freed during his inaugural address, Mike Deaver would slip him a note. He wanted to be able to publicly acknowledge Carter's efforts and ultimate achievement. "No country should embarrass and humiliate the president of the United States," he said.[14]

For acknowledgment to have its full effect, its greatest value, empowering others to peak performance, leaders must be in rapport with their associates. They must have credibility. You create this rapport first of all by paying attention when teammates show up, finding ways to greet and acknowledge team members for being at their places.

Give effective approval for honest effort, and demonstrate appreciation to those who go the extra mile. Your praise focuses on qualities like self-discipline, determination, dedication, and other character traits that drive your team to peak performance. Empowering leaders make a point of lending support when others are down. They are proactive in building up the morale of everyone on the team by looking for every opportunity to give acknowledgment.

You will be at your best when you adopt this practice of giving credit to others. If you are a sales manager, remember to share the credit for exceptional sales increases with engineering and production. When you acknowledge other members of your team, you go a long way toward being an empowering leader.

———

When President Reagan took office he knew that the public image of the American military, both as individuals and as a profession, had suffered greatly in recent decades and needed to be changed. Reagan always saluted the troops, even though military protocol dictated that he should not salute unless his head was covered. He changed this tradition, taking pride in every opportunity to acknowledge the service and sacrifices of members of the armed forces.[15]

Former Secretary of State Colin Powell,

chairman of the Joint Chiefs of Staff under Reagan, recalled a time early in Reagan's presidency that a young Army paratrooper asked him to tell the president that Reagan's support meant a lot to all in uniform.[16] Concerning the salute, Powell told Reagan, "Mr. President, please don't ever stop."[17]

"The president exercised vital leadership here," wrote former Secretary of Defense Caspar Weinberger, "making numerous appearances at military events and posts, praising, with his characteristic warmth and patriotism, the men and women in uniform who are willing to sacrifice their lives for their country. This helped enormously in changing the public's perception of our armed forces into one of deep appreciation and respect. It also helped raise the morale of the troops themselves, and that improved recruiting."[18]

One of Reagan's most eloquent tributes to American servicemen was delivered at the U.S. Ranger Monument at Pointe du Hoc, Normandy on the fortieth anniversary of D-Day. In the presence of World War II veterans, he said:

"We stand on a lonely, windswept point on the northern shore of France. The air is soft, but forty years ago at this moment, the air was dense with smoke and the cries of men, and the air was filled with the crack of rifle fire and the roar of cannon....

"Behind me is a memorial that symbolizes the Ranger daggers that were thrust into the top of these cliffs. And before me are the men who put them there.

"These are the boys of Pointe du Hoc. These are the men who took the cliffs. These are the champions who helped free a continent. These are the heroes who helped end a war.

"Gentlemen, I look at you and I think of the words of Stephen Spender's poem. You are men who in your lives 'fought for life...and left the vivid air signed with your honor....'"[19]

In your role as leader you have occasion to look back on the achievements of your team, be they a week ago or decades. Take the occasions to show appreciation for past and present team members. Look beyond the usual everyday occasions to extend credit to the families of your associates, to suppliers, to strategic partners, to customers, to any and all who are involved in your success. You never know how much your appreciation means to others or who will be touched by it.

My uncle was one of the young men who stormed the beaches of Normandy. He never understood the meaning of the sacrifices he and his friends made in 1944 or felt they were significant. He told me that when he heard Ronald Reagan's speech at Pointe du Hoc forty years later, it changed his perspective immeasurably. President Reagan's expressions of gratitude on behalf of the nation and of a liberated Europe gave my uncle—and no doubt thousands of other veterans in their twilight years—a renewed belief in himself and in his important part in history.

———

George H. W. Bush said, "There are countless examples of [Reagan's] many kindnesses to the people around him. He never walked by a doorman or elevator operator or groundskeeper at the White House without acknowledging that person and making them feel warm and welcome."[20]

Reagan took the time to thank people for things he appreciated, whether the favor was public or private. He called his speechwriter Peggy Noonan to thank her personally for the speech she wrote for him on the spur of the moment when the *Challenger* space shuttle exploded, the worst disaster in NASA's history. She wrote the speech as soon as she heard about the tragedy, knowing the president would want to give an address to the nation.

Because Noonan had written the speech so quickly, under the stress of the moment, she was afraid it would be a failure. In fact, millions of Americans were touched by the *Challenger* speech, which remains one of Ronald Reagan's most famous speeches. The president did not have to call and thank her. After all, she had only done her job. But he wanted to say thank you, and his appreciation meant a lot to her. [21]

Agent Tim McCarthy was also doing his job when he shielded the president and took a bullet during the assassination attempt of March 30, 1981. He helped saved Reagan's life, and the president made sure McCarthy and his family knew how grateful he was. Reagan said to him, "Someday I hope your children will know what a brave father they have." He wrote to McCarthy's children, telling them what he thought of their father.[22]

Early in Reagan's first term he asked Ambassador to the United Nations Jeane Kirkpatrick to negotiate a difficult resolution condemning the Israeli bombing of an Iraqi nuclear reactor without making it look as if the U.S. were wavering in its support of Israel. The president was so pleased with her achieving his objective that Kirkpatrick said, "At the next Cabinet meeting, he put his arm around me and called me his 'heroine'—which of course delighted me." "I found him to be very generous with praise," she added.[23]

Empowering leaders do not assume others know how much they appreciate what they do. They tell them.

In a 1978 radio address Ronald Reagan recalled a time when he unexpectedly found himself on the receiving end of someone's acknowledgment and praise. This occurred during the student uprisings at the University of California at San Diego. Governor Reagan arrived for a meeting of the Board of Regents and was met by a demonstration of over a thousand students. He walked two hundred yards to the building, the silent protesters giving him barely enough room to pass.

"I was almost to the end of the ordeal," said Reagan, "when a rather small, attractive, blonde girl stepped out of the crowd and stood on the walk facing me. I thought 'Oh Dear Lord what have they planned for me now.' But she put out her hand and spoke, her voice ringing like a bell in all that deep silence. She said 'I just want to tell you I like everything you are doing.' I took her hand but I couldn't thank her, there was a baseball-size lump in my throat.

"I've never forgotten that moment and her courage. I could go on into the building; she had to stay out there with her peers. I never found out who she was. I'd like to tell her what her bravery meant to me. I'd like to say thanks."[24] He always wished he had been able to reciprocate her appreciation of him.

———

Reagan never stopped giving acknowledgment, never stopped saying thank you. His son Ron recalled an incident from late in his father's life. "There's a particular Secret Service agent, an African-American man," he said. "This guy is a big, burly guy who looked like he played football. When my father was still able to get up and on his feet and sort of be walked to the living room and put in a chair, this guy would be on one side of him and another agent on the other. My father would often not want to let go of his hand....

"He couldn't verbalize anything at that point....But he looked at the agent.

"Then he took his hand and kissed it."[25]

People express encouragement and praise in different ways. Take some time to identify how you can effectively give praise and encouragement. Empowering leaders know how far a little appreciation goes in boosting the morale of their team. They take and make every opportunity to give empowering praise.

Leadership Principle 5

"East and West do not mistrust each other because we are armed; we are armed because we mistrust each other."

Ronald Reagan[1]

See Their Point of View

During the 1976 presidential primary, Ronald Reagan gave a speech in a North Carolina parking lot. California Congressman Dana Rohrabacher, formerly Reagan's assistant press secretary, recalled that a woman asked Reagan to come say hello to a group of blind children after the speech.

"There were six or seven kids...about eight or nine years old," said Rohrabacher. "...Reagan bent down, close to the kids, to talk to them. But somehow I could see him thinking that that wasn't enough. So after the kids had asked him a couple of questions, he said, '...Would you like to touch my face so you can get a better understanding of how I look?' The kids all smiled and said yes, so Reagan just leaned over into them, and one by one these

91

little kids began moving their fingers over his face to see what he looked like."[2]

Reagan never felt it was beneath his dignity to put himself in another's shoes, to see the world through their eyes. He looked for ways to communicate with others, understanding that each person is unique. He was not embarrassed by differences and made others feel at ease.

Understanding another's point of view is crucial for success in gaining cooperation and leading from strength. Empowering leaders endeavor to consider all the differences that may set them apart from others, with an eye toward better understanding what they have in common. They consider others' background, upbringing, experiences, education, character traits, and capacity. They take into account their challenges, needs, interests, the kinds of organizations in which they have worked, positions they have held, and what their personal relationships are or have been. They want to know what conclusions others have reached about work, their philosophy, and values.

———

"I am familiar with your Constitution," Mikhail Gorbachev told Nancy Reagan in their

1988 visit to the USSR, "but I wish your husband could stay on for another four years." "It was fascinating to hear," Mrs. Reagan wrote. "While it's possible he was being polite, I believe he was sincere. He and Ronnie had developed a mutual respect and affection."[3]

Coming from completely different world-views, Reagan and Gorbachev came to a genuine mutual respect and regard for each other.

In *An American Life*, Reagan wrote that his early drama training helped him learn how to get into the other person's shoes, to see the world through their eyes. His high school English teacher encouraged students to think like the characters they were trying to portray. He asked Reagan to think about why his characters said what they did and what the characters meant by it. Reagan learned the importance of getting to know his characters and to understand their motivations.

"After a while," Reagan wrote, "whenever I read a new script, I'd automatically try first to understand what made that particular human being tick by trying to put myself in his place. The process, called empathy, is not bad training for someone who goes into politics (or any other calling). By developing a knack for putting yourself in someone else's shoes, it helps you relate better to others and perhaps understand why they think as they do, even though they come from a background much different from yours."[4]

Empowering leaders want to know the other person's world-view and understand how deeply their attitudes, feelings, and conclusions run. They treat each person differently, respectfully, in light of their nature, mindset, and viewpoint. Seeing things from another's point of view does not require surrendering your perspective, objectives, or values. Rather, it means seeing the world as the other person sees it. This allows you to exercise empathy. Until we understand the other person, there can be no true communication. If you treat everyone the same way, you will not be treating most people the right way.

Above all else, you want respect from your team. It is nice to be liked. Some managers want to be loved. There are even managers still trying to rely on fear to "lead" others. These approaches are not sustainable or even desirable in our dynamic, changing world. To lead you must earn the respect of all your associates. It is essential. You go a long way toward earning respect by seeing others' perspective, their point of view, and treating each person as a unique individual.

———

Despite his successful career Ronald Reagan never lost touch with his working-class roots. Because of his family's experiences in the early twentieth century, Reagan understood the thinking behind FDR's New Deal and why people still supported these government programs he believed had grown too large and wasteful. Reagan grew up in poverty and was unemployed during the Depression. He worked to achieve his dreams, aspiring to be a radio announcer, then a Hollywood actor, governor of California, and eventually president of the United States. Reagan believed everyone could become "someone" because he himself was a "nobody."[5]

Reagan showed he cared about others' point of view by working hard to make sure he understood it. For eight years, from 1954 to 1962, Reagan was the principal spokesman for General Electric. In this capacity he spoke to over 250,000 GE employees and listened to their concerns. This experience gave him direct information about workers' problems, needs, and concerns within GE's many diversified industries.

Empowering leaders put themselves in the other person's shoes. Before making recommendations, proposals, or decisions, they consider how changes in policies or procedures will impact their associates' lives. An example would be changes in the health plan that require employees to contribute more to the co-pay. What effect will this have on employees' budgets and their families? Likewise, changing hours, routines, or locations have ramifications for employees which empowering leaders take time to foresee.

The best salespeople are not pushing for a sale. Instead, they endeavor to gain a deep understanding of what the customer is really looking for, what problem they want to solve. Empowering leaders are in tune with how others feel living with a problem they could help solve. They are motivated by how their associates will feel when the obstacles or difficulties are overcome and the pain subsides.

———

From Hollywood to the White House, Reagan cultivated the habit of trying to understand others' point of view, to empathize with them. As previously mentioned, Reagan was an avid correspondent. Former aide Nancy Clark Reynolds said that Reagan saw a parallel between the fan mail he received as a movie star and the letters from concerned citizens he received as governor and as president. As an actor, he owed his career to those who came to see his films; as governor and president, he owed his office to the voters.[6] He took time to read and answer as many letters as possible.[7] As president, Reagan referred to the "ordinary" Americans to whom he wrote as "uncommon" people. Reynolds said that Reagan "was willing to talk to anybody," "was willing to write to anybody."[8]

Often Reagan would hand-write and seal his letters himself to add an even more personal touch. Just a few days after his inauguration, the White House Post Office notified Anne Higgins, director of the Correspondence Unit, that someone was using the president's stationery. She discovered that the president himself was already engaged in correspondence with Americans who wrote to offer advice, criticism, or their personal stories.[9]

In his letters, Reagan was respectful of differences, explaining his position without discounting the other's perspective. He thanked people for their concern and for expressing their ideas, even if he disagreed with them. He liked to elaborate on his own thinking if he had the time and often concluded with another thank-you. He never talked down to people. Instead, he raised them up by offering information he thought they would appreciate. "He had the ability to talk to people at whatever their level without patronizing them," said Lou Cannon.[10]

For example, in 1988 he responded to a class of third-graders. He thanked them for their letters and said he had read them all. He geared his letter to their level. He explained briefly how he used to be a Democrat, described the White House, answered their questions, and offered some facts about the Constitution and some details of the president's life that children would find interesting.[11] Such a letter was not uncommon for Reagan.

Not only did Reagan spend time on letters to hear what the "uncommon" people were thinking, he was conscious of the point of view of his personal staff. Anne Higgins recalled that Reagan "was a secretary's dream." Aware of the volume of his secretaries' work, he made their job easier and less time-consuming by writing the addressee's name, address, zip code, and telephone number, if he had them, on the correspondence they were to type.[12]

When we see the other person's point of view, we do not cause downstream associates unnecessary work. Our hand-offs are always more seamless and the enterprise runs more effectively.

———

"[Reagan] took obvious delight in the give-and-take of ideas," said writer and editor R.

Emmett Tyrrell, Jr.[13] As a leader in Sacramento and in Washington, Reagan was proactive in encouraging his advisors to speak up and offer their perspectives. He told his cabinet to tell him whatever they were thinking about any topic under consideration, even if it did not involve their own department. He wanted to know their reservations as well as their ideas, whether they supported something or not.[14] He knew that the more he listened to the team, the greater his perspective would be and the better informed they would all be. Ultimately, better decisions would be made.

Empowering leaders strive to create an environment where all points of view are freely aired. They ensure that no one holds back, that all parties and interests are heard. If some on your team are concerned about giving up key personnel or other resources, be sure you understand their perspective. If they feel a department is being shortchanged, a process can be improved, or a market more successfully exploited, seek to fully understand their vision.

———

In 1981, Vice President Bush recorded in his private diary that the president respected his input and made him feel comfortable giving it. They met for a private lunch every Thursday, a tradition Bush continued with Dan Quayle during his own presidency. Bush wrote that Reagan was "a great joke teller, and the most understanding human being....[H]e makes you feel totally relaxed....I feel uninhibited in bringing things up to him."[15] Reagan invited the input of his team members by creating a White House environment in which they found it easy to talk to him.

Speaker of the House Tip O'Neill once called Mike Deaver to express his objection to the name *Corpus Christi* for a Navy submarine. He explained that "Corpus Christi" is Latin for "the Body of Christ," and he asked Deaver to tell the president he felt the name was inappropriate. Deaver spoke to Reagan, who thought O'Neill's concern sounded reasonable. Reagan called Secretary of Defense Caspar Weinberger and suggested that the submarine be called *City of Corpus Christi*. O'Neill was gratified that the president took his point of view seriously.[16]

Reagan's respect for others' input extended to foreign leaders as well. He particularly valued Prime Minister Margaret Thatcher's perspective. He asked her for it, even when he knew he would have to pursue a different course. In her memoir *The Downing Street Years*, Lady Thatcher recalled Reagan's request for her thoughts and advice on the pending American intervention in Grenada. She strongly opposed American intervention. However, Reagan and Thatcher had cultivated a close consultative relationship, so their friendship (both as allies and personally) ultimately was undamaged.[17]

This is a great example of asking for a perspective you know in advance will be different from your own. Even if you know you will be unable to accept the other position or reconcile it with your own, understanding all angles under these circumstances can be even more valuable. There are often considerations you will not ever think of without the help of someone who sees things from a different point of view. Although you may have to agree to disagree, seeing the other person's point of view can strengthen your relationship and deepen your understanding of each other's needs, concerns, and values.

Seeing the other person's point of view, even when you cannot reconcile the two perspectives, is real diversity. When this kind of diversity is embraced, you realize there are not two sides, or even four sides, to a story. Rather than seeing two sides of a coin, you will come to understand that most situations are more like many-faceted diamonds. When you look at all the facets, you have deeper understanding, real communication, reach better conclusions, and make more informed decisions.

———

At the 1976 convention, having lost the presidential nomination to Gerald Ford, Reagan refused to take the stage without Ford personally inviting him from the microphone. He did not want his presence to detract from Ford's night. Ford did publicly call Reagan to join him on stage and give a spur-of-the-moment speech. Reagan gave one of the best speeches of his life, in front of the biggest audience yet.[18] His insistence on seeing the situation from Ford's viewpoint turned out to be the best possible thing for Reagan. Four years later, he was the nominee.

An empowering leader who works to see the other person's point of view takes every opportunity to be aware of the other's needs and to make the other person look good. Reagan did not just look out for his interest; in looking out for others he demonstrated his strength.

———

Reagan received harsh criticism for his appearance at a military cemetery in Bitburg, West Germany in 1985. He was scheduled to commemorate the fortieth anniversary of the end of World War II, and the subsequent friendship of Germany and the U.S., by joining Chancellor Helmut Kohl in a wreath-laying ceremony.[19]

Many were offended when it was discovered that Nazi storm troopers were among those buried in the cemetery. Because of snow, it was hard to know for sure where the Nazi graves were and if they were close to the wreath-laying site. When the event became a potential embarrassment for Reagan, his staff wanted to change the itinerary.

Reagan refused to back out, believing he should follow through on his commitment to Chancellor Kohl. Kohl was afraid that if Reagan did not come, it would appear he was being snubbed by the president of the United States. Kohl's fragile administration would be undermined. Given the political situation in Europe, that could have harmed the stability of free West Germany.

Reagan took a lot of heat for the appearance at Bitburg, even though Matt Ridgway, the last living four-star general involved in the European theater, voluntarily joined Reagan at the cemetery to diffuse criticism.[20] Chancellor Kohl was grateful to the president for saving his face. Reagan demonstrated character as a leader by not abandoning an ally.[21]

Reagan showed strength of character by considering everyone's perspectives and then choosing to do what he believed he had committed to do. Rather than doing what was expedient, he followed through with the decision he had already made in order to support Chancellor Kohl. Sometimes a leader makes decisions based on limited information, as Reagan did at Bitburg. An empowering leader weighs commitments against other considerations to determine the principled course of action.

———

On March 30, 1981, Reagan arrived at George Washington University Hospital after being shot outside the Washington Hilton. He got out of the car unaided, buttoned his suit jacket, and walked several steps to the hospital door before collapsing inside. He did not know yet that he had been shot, but he felt an excruciating pain in his chest. He guessed he had broken a rib while being thrown into the car after shots rang out at the hotel. He knew a frightened American public would be reassured by seeing the president walk into the hospital unaided to get himself checked over.

By providing this last public image before his life-saving surgery, Reagan strikingly proved his empathy with Americans. He knew that America and the world were watching and wondering what was going on with the president. He understood people's need to be reassured, even when he was the one in trouble. He realized the importance of his health from the perspective of Americans at home and the world community abroad.

The morning after Reagan's surgery, his staff brought him a bill to sign. He approved of this small but powerful gesture, demonstrating to Americans that the president was still functioning. It boosted everyone's confidence. Former presidential advisor Lyn Nofziger wrote that Reagan had always "talked the good fight to all Americans," but no one knew how he would handle a major crisis.[22] Nofziger was the one who recorded Reagan's emergency room jokes. "When I later reported them to the press," he wrote, "the nation knew that everything would be all right."[23]

Despite his own precarious physical condition, Reagan saw the situation through the eyes of a traumatized nation. He understood Americans' fear and sought to reassure them with his humor and small gestures.

An empowering leader is in tune with the anxiety and stress experienced by departments within their organization, which face their own unique challenges. New competition, lost financing, lost clientele, lost suppliers, and other factors common in a changing market can have a straining effect on your team. Often empowering leaders must make their own feelings subservient to the common good of their team to prevent the spread of discouragement or a negative atmosphere. Putting on an optimistic face during hard times can lift the morale of your team. It can actually improve the chances of success of the entire enterprise, as you encourage your team to overcome fear, doubt, and discouragement.

———

Empowering leaders know where others are coming from in order to maximize everyone's contributions. They know the perspective of employees, coworkers, investors, and certainly customers.

It takes dedication and effort to get to know your team members' points of view. Seeing others' points of view requires uncovering their ideas, concerns, fears, and vision. When you practice empathy you show your respect for others by putting forth the effort to develop meaningful working relationships. You build mutual trust, promote understanding, combat fear and negativity, and become a more empowering leader. In the final analysis, you gain two major advantages: You gain information, perspective, and insight that greatly help you in your decision-making; and you gain the respect, loyalty, and trust of your team.

Leadership Principle 6

"No matter where I was, I'd find people...waiting to talk to me after a speech and they'd all say, 'Hey, if you think things are bad in your business, let me tell you what is happening in my business....' I'd listen...."

Ronald Reagan[1]

Be an Active Listener

In 1987 President Reagan called a twenty-nine-year-old staff member named Doug MacKinnon to thank him for some good work he had done. MacKinnon wrote presidential messages and made video greetings for the White House correspondence office. Reagan invited MacKinnon to drop by the Oval Office and introduce himself in person. When MacKinnon came in, he found the president so friendly that he spontaneously told Reagan, "Mr. President, my father has the same thing your father had," meaning alcoholism.

Reagan immediately understood, leaning forward in his seat to listen while the young man explained how difficult it had been growing up with his father's problem. MacKinnon knew the president understood everything. "All the things you've just mentioned happened to me," Reagan told him.

MacKinnon later said: "To have him spend time out of an incredibly busy schedule to talk about an issue that was still so big for me, so burdensome—it meant the world to me. That he could persevere and become what he became—to be the son or daughter of an alcoholic is a tough lifestyle to make it out of and many people don't, but he did. I was able to move on and it was because of one man's kindness."[2] Reagan's taking the opportunity to listen and empathize changed MacKinnon's life.

Perhaps the most powerful need of the human heart is to be heard; and many, if not most, of us never feel fully heard. The leader who listens has the power to change not just performance but the direction of a life for eternity.

Empowering leaders are active listeners and encourage others to talk about themselves. They ask questions, and as they actively listen, they uncover attitudes and ideas that otherwise might not be heard. Great leaders have learned to make a fine art of listening. They know that listening is far more than mere silence.

Not only do they take a genuine interest in what people are saying, they actively demonstrate their interest through such telltale signs as focused eye-contact, nodding, and leaning forward. They offer verbal encouragement: "That must have been... (interesting, challenging, frustrating, etc.). How did you do that? What happened next? What do you think caused that?" Yes, active listening is more than waiting for a break so you can jump in. Active listening draws the other person out.

When we set aside our own feelings, attitudes, likes, dislikes, and prejudices, and let the feelings, attitudes, likes, dislikes, prejudices, and opinions of others speak to us, we learn to understand the other person. Through this understanding, we learn to communicate in meaningful ways.

Mastering listening skills requires hearing beyond words and understanding the feelings that lie beneath the words. You protect and nourish successful relationships when you listen at depth. You will master active listening through practice and patience. Be as active and engaged when you listen as when you speak.

———

Empowering leaders know that those closest to the work have insights which can improve all processes in the enterprise. These insights must be solicited, listened to, and acted upon. These expert members of the team, who have "Ph.D.'s in experience," can provide the insights and advantage that is required to win in an increasingly competitive worldwide market.

While representing General Electric, Ronald Reagan traveled to each of GE's 135 plants.[3] Listening to these employees describe their experiences in the American work force, Reagan learned about their concerns, needs, challenges, and triumphs. He believed that listening is the invaluable trait of an empowering leader.

Ronald Reagan, wrote Mike Deaver, "was genuine and a good listener, not typical traits for a politician."[4] Reagan actively cultivated the art of listening. When running for governor of California, he proved his ability to listen and his interest in what people had to say by giving an unusual kind of "speech."

Having been accused of being out of touch, of merely reading speeches other people prepared for him, Reagan chose to have a "dialogue" rather than to give a "speech."[5] Reagan briefly made his opening remarks and then opened the floor to questions from his listeners. He was good at this, largely because he spent nearly a decade interacting in this way with GE employees. He later employed this same technique with great success when running for president.[6]

Reagan knew how to connect with an

audience and would not let anything get in the way of their participation. He directed his aides not to dim the lights when he spoke because he did not want those in attendance to feel like an audience—passively sitting in their chairs, watching a show on a spotlighted stage. "He liked to see into their eyes," wrote Mike Deaver, "to gauge the effectiveness of his words and movements."[7]

Reagan was nearsighted, but he did not let that get in the way of connecting with his audience. In the early days of contact lenses, he discovered a compromise between wearing his contacts to see the audience or taking them out to read his speech. He kept the right contact in and the left one out, rigging his own "bifocals," so he could do both.[8] He knew it was as important for him to read his audience as it was to read his speech.

Empowering leaders are always watching to see how they are being taken, if they are getting through, if their message is coming across. They make others feel included in a dialogue and relevant to the debate. Active listening involves more than your ears; it means using your eyes to take in the entire scene around you.

Reagan tried to carry over this conversational aspect of public speaking even to television appearances. He wrote: "I try to remember that audiences are made up of individuals, and I try to speak as if I am talking to a group of friends...not to millions, but to a handful of people in a living room...or a barbershop."[9]

Reagan knew that in question-and-answer "speeches," the audience was not just learning about Ronald Reagan. Ronald Reagan was learning about the individuals there, their concerns, the details of their lives, the various aspects of their work. He said he came away from each session "a smarter man," more in tune with the experiences of average Americans.[10]

Empowering leaders know that communication is a two-way street. They learn as much by listening to their audience as their audience does by listening to them. Never underestimate the value of the feedback you get from your team, customers, suppliers, and peers. Listen to what they have to say. Show your genuine interest in them by listening actively and attentively.

The monthly, quarterly, and annual state of the enterprise reports given by managers can be dramatically improved simply by initiating a dialogue. Ask your team how they improved certain scores and what their plans are for continuing improvement. Take questions about any issue—don't have sacred cows. Listen to concerns about the future of the enterprise and their part in it. Set aside any inclination or temptation to be defensive. You will be surprised at how much you learn.

———

Reagan was widely considered a great listener. David Laux, director of Asian Affairs for the National Security Council, said: "I was always impressed with the president's sensitivity to everyone who was in a meeting with him. If he saw anyone there who seemed anxious to say something, he figured it must be important, so [he] drew it out."[11] He made sure that he heard everyone's views.[12] Reagan's staff quickly learned that the president paid close attention to what they told him. They knew that they had to get their facts straight because he would indeed remember what they said. He prepared for meetings, asked hard questions, and listened closely to their answers.[13]

In many meetings and on most teams there will be a few—20%—who will do most of the talking. Watch for the soft-spoken introverts to indicate they are ready to contribute and draw them out: "What do you think?" "How would you handle this?" "What is your opinion?"

"What would you do?" These can be good questions to prime the pump and help them get started.

———

Former Speaker of the House Tip O'Neill wrote in his memoir, *Man of the House*, that some Democratic members of Congress saw more of Reagan in the first four months of Reagan's term than they had seen of the last president (a member of their own party) in the duration of his presidency. Reagan "didn't always get his way," said O'Neill, "but his calls were never wasted....The members adored it when he called, even when they had no intention of changing their vote. The men and women in Congress love nothing better than to hear from the head guy, so they can go back to their districts and say, 'I was talking to the president the other day.' The constituents love it, too, because they want to believe that their representative is important enough to be in touch with the chief."[14]

Former presidential chief of staff Kenneth Duberstein wrote that Reagan often called members of Congress "not just to lobby them, but to find out what was going on in their districts....That flattered [them] and gave the President contact with the mood of the country."[15]

How about the associates on your team who would like to be able to say to their spouses or to coworkers in the break room or in a team meeting, "When I was talking with the 'president' (manager) the other day..."? Give them that opportunity by being available. Don't underestimate the positive effect this has on morale.

Too many managers rely on reports to tell them how their team members are doing. Empowering leaders know that they learn more about the heartbeat of the organization by literally walking around than they could ever learn by staying isolated and relying on statistical reports and other formal feedback. In one-on-one contact where the mission of your organization is being carried out, you pick up "by osmosis" what you otherwise might miss about the strengths and weaknesses of your team.

By listening to your associates directly, you gain a better understanding of your team members, what is working, and what is missing a beat or broken. Your office is a dangerous place from which to run your company. By wandering around, you are in a much better position to listen to others' ideas and concerns. You invite their input with your presence and open the door to dialogue.

———

A major test of President Reagan's leadership was whether or not Congress embraced his agenda. Reagan knew that his relationship with individual members of Congress was crucial to achieving his goals, so he initiated a dialogue with Democrats as individuals. Doing so demonstrated that he respected them enough to give them the opportunity to have a voice. The personal relationships he formed in Congress helped get more done in areas like tax reform and a balanced budget than anyone, Democrat or Republican, had dreamed was possible. And always in negotiation, Reagan said to biographer Lou Cannon, "[i]t pays to *listen* to what they are offering."[16]

Empowering leaders are called to champion change. Change is never easy. Many see change as a loss. You can help alter this perception by connecting with as many people as possible one-on-one before the change is formally announced and implemented, securing understanding and support.

Dialogue skills are among the most important skills of an empowering leader. It is through successful dialogue that you come to understand others' concerns and perspective. An empowering leader gains understanding through "deep listening." Develop the habit of saying, "Tell me more about that," "How would that work?" "How do you mean that?" or "Why do you feel that way?" Ask, "Has that happened lately?" Use questions to seek out the other person's input and point of view. Maximize your most important sources of information by being a proactive listener.

———

It speaks well of Reagan as a leader that he was open to listening to the unsolicited advice of his staff and welcomed their input, especially during difficult times. During the Israeli bombing of Beirut, Lebanon, Mike Deaver expressed to Reagan his own troubled conscience over the situation. He reminded the president that he had the power to call Prime Minister Menachem Begin and say the bombing needed to stop. To Deaver's surprise, Reagan immediately did just that. Reagan had been feeling the same way, and listening to another person articulate his gut assessment of the situation helped Reagan to make his decision as a leader.[17]

"In any top position," Reagan wrote, "you risk becoming isolated: People tell you what you want to hear....Not many people close to you are

118

willing to say: *You're wrong.*" He appreciated it when those close to him gave advice and listened to what they had to say, especially his wife Nancy.[18]

If your team knows you to be a good listener, they will be more willing to offer the valuable input you need and want to make your enterprise a success. Maximize the power of your team by inviting their comments and encouraging them to air their concerns. Too many good ideas are never acted upon because they did not see the light of day. Make it safe for controversial ideas to be suggested, including all of the out-of-the-box "what if?" questions.

Here are seven steps you can take to become a better listener. 1) Find areas of interest—be on the alert for learning something new. 2) Judge content, not delivery—pay more attention to ideas than to how well or poorly they are expressed. 3) Listen for ideas—look for central themes. 4) Be flexible—set aside prejudices and preconceived conclusions about the subject at hand. 5) Exercise your mind—engage your thinking skills as you listen. 6) Keep your mind open—do not get hung up on emotional words. 7) Capitalize on fact; thought is faster than speech. Challenge yourself to stay focused, anticipate what you will learn, and listen to the speaker's tone of voice for clues: conviction, uncertainty, fear, doubt, confidence, determination.

People have no idea how much their listening means to others. Knowing that your views and concerns are heard makes all the difference in the world. When a leader cannot change a policy or right a wrong done, empathetic listening goes a long way toward improving morale. Do not underestimate the power of stopping by to see how your team is doing. You strengthen their self-esteem and help yourself understand them and win their hearts. Your enterprise will be more profitable, and it is more than making money. Engaged listening can make their day, and yours as well.

Leadership Principle 7

When asked if he would consider running for president, Reagan replied, "What's the matter—don't you like my acting either?"[1]

Play Yourself Down ~ Exercise Humility

During the 1980 presidential campaign, former Democratic Senator Eugene McCarthy, "one of the most respected liberals to ever serve in the Senate," requested a private meeting with Ronald Reagan in Iowa. Wrote Mike Deaver, "I couldn't understand why this icon of the left would want to meet with the new Mr. Conservative, especially during a heated campaign." McCarthy stunned Deaver by explaining that he wanted to endorse Ronald Reagan for president.

"'I'll tell you why,' he said....'It's because he is the only man since Harry Truman who won't confuse the job with the man.'"[2]

Ronald Reagan, wrote his wife Nancy, "never looked at his position in terms of 'I am president.' Instead, he would refer to the

121

presidency as 'the office I now hold,' or even 'this job.'...For Ronnie, it would have been presumptuous to view his job in any other way.

"Perhaps the fact that Ronnie never equated the presidency with himself helps to explain why he wasn't worn down by the pressures and disappointments of the office."[3]

An integral part of empowering leadership, earning respect, and building trust is your willingness to play yourself down. This presupposes a humble attitude that says to those around you, "My title may give me more sway than others, yet I realize it is the organization that gave me the title. Without the organization and the people who make it up, who would I be?" In a word, playing yourself down requires humility. Humility is a quality that only the truly self-confident can honestly display.

———

"Ronald Reagan was interested in ideas, not in Ronald Reagan," wrote former White House Counsel Peter Wallison.[4] One of the first things people mention who personally knew Ronald Reagan is that he was a humble, gracious man. He did not feel he had to prove anything to anyone. He did not show off or put himself forward. Mike Deaver agreed: "Ronald Reagan thought that Ronald Reagan was the most boring topic in the world."[5] "In a let-it-all-hang-out age, America found itself being led, ironically, by a man who really couldn't stand to talk about himself."[6]

Strong, competent leaders who willingly play themselves down are leaders whom others eagerly raise up. When acting as the leader, convincing others to carry out your plans, whenever possible keep yourself in the background. Avoid pretension of any kind. A joke on yourself is often an effective means of playing yourself down while disarming any defensiveness or hostility. Be ready to sacrifice your vanity when you choose assistants and friends, and be able to play yourself down when you interact with them.

———

"Reagan wasn't just comfortable in his own skin," wrote presidential advisor David Gergen in *Eyewitness to Power*. "He was serene. And he had a clear sense of what he was trying to accomplish. Those were among his greatest strengths as a leader....He knew where he wanted to go and how he might get there."[7] Empowering leaders know who they are—know themselves—and are crystal clear about their intentions, their mission, and their vision for the future.

"What's the secret of Ronald Reagan's immense success?" asked Deaver. "The guy knows who he is. In the public relations business, I constantly tell clients—corporations or candidates, it doesn't matter—if you don't know who you are, there's not a lot I can do for you."[8]

Deaver recalled walking with Reagan in New York City, when Reagan was governor of California. A man mistook Reagan for actor Ray Milland and eagerly asked for his autograph, saying, "Please, Mr. Milland." Reagan signed, "Mr. Milland." When Deaver asked why he didn't tell the man he was Ronald Reagan, governor of California, he replied good-humoredly, "Why? I know who I am."[9] He felt no need to impress or to assert his ego.[10] He did not embarrass the autograph-seeker.

Empowering leaders are confident in the face of challenge, poised in crises, unruffled when attacked. They feel secure being themselves and so have no need for pretense or posturing. When you know who you are, you do not feel the need to puff yourself up by correcting others on fine points. You don't always have to be right. You can play yourself down while shining the light on the vision and mission of your organization.

———

Reagan chose not to always be the focus of attention. He would redirect attention from himself toward others. In 1981 he gave the commencement address at the University of Notre Dame. "I am the fifth President to address a Notre Dame commencement," he said. "The temptation is great to use this forum for an address on some national or international issue having nothing to do with the occasion itself. Indeed this is somewhat traditional so I haven't been surprised to read in a number of reputable journals that I was going to deliver a major address on foreign policy. Others said it would be on the economy. It will be on neither."[11]

Reagan's address challenged the students to aim for excellence. He did not use the opportunity to grandstand, to focus on himself or on his importance as president of the United States. Instead, he focused on the good they could do as leaders in their corners of the world.

Nancy Reagan often recalls her husband's self-effacing way. She described her first meeting with him in *My Turn*: "One of the things I liked about Ronnie right away was that he didn't talk only about himself. I had been out on dates with a number of actors, and all the conversations were pretty much the same: his first picture, his second picture, his most recent picture, his current picture, his next picture.

"But this man was different. His world was not limited to himself or his career. He told me about the Guild, and why the actors' union meant so much to him. He talked about his small ranch in the San Fernando Valley...; he was also a Civil War buff, and he knew a lot about wine."[12]

Our achievements can look so big in our eyes. We become "legends" in our own minds. Empowering leaders do not focus on themselves and their achievements. Rather, they play themselves down while playing up the accomplishments of others.

———

When Reagan was recovering in the hospital after the 1981 assassination attempt, Vice President Bush caught the leader of the free world mopping the floor with a towel. The president explained that he had spilled water washing his face and did not want the nurse to get in trouble, since he was not supposed to be out of bed.

Ed Meese said in an interview that he thought "the great thing about Ronald Reagan is that he took his work seriously, he took his job seriously, but he didn't take *himself* seriously...."[13]

Respect for your position is a way of

playing yourself down while adding stature to the position itself. Reagan had a profound respect for the office of the presidency, famously illustrated by his refusal to remove his suit jacket in the Oval Office, even during the hot and humid Washington summers. But as Senator McCarthy observed, Reagan did not confuse the office with the man. While he was careful to have his personal behavior reflect the dignity of the presidency, he did not take himself too seriously.

Your position gives you authority. Don't flaunt it or try to impress people with who you are. A little humility goes a long way toward earning the respect that is so essential to leadership. If you let your position, your title, or your accomplishments get to you, you lose touch with your humanity. It can happen at any level from the new lead, supervisor, or assistant manager to the new company president. If you succumb to the temptation and flaunt your ego, you may live to regret it. Keep your humility, and others will want to emulate you, respect you, and follow you enthusiastically.

———

Courtesy was important to Reagan. Consequently, he disliked the way presidential security got in the way of his usual good manners. In her book *When Character Was King*, Peggy Noonan recounted Reagan's friend Marion Jorgensen's memories of election night, 1980. When the Reagans arrived at her house for a party, Mrs. Jorgensen was surprised to see the president-elect get out of the car before his wife. Reagan always followed Nancy; but now the Secret Service insisted that for his safety, the president had to exit the vehicle first. Reagan told Mrs. Jorgensen that he hated having to get out of the car "before any woman, before Nancy."[14]

Necessary security precautions never went to Reagan's head. "It's just hard to believe," Mrs. Jorgensen said. "Nothing ever changed him. He was always the same. He had humility, he didn't think he was better than anyone else."[15]

Former First Lady Barbara Bush told a story about a time Lee Annenberg, the White House chief of protocol, instructed President and Mrs. Reagan to enter a room, followed by Vice President and Mrs. Bush. When they actually entered the room, Reagan ignored the instruction, stepping back and saying, "After you, Barbara. Ladies first."[16]

You may not have thought of manners as a way of playing yourself down, yet they are. Manners are a way of deferring to others. Much of what used to be considered common courtesy seems to have gone by the way. You can differentiate yourself and earn the respect of others through the practice of courtesy: opening the door, letting others go first, saying please and thank you. Manners show that you are thinking of others before yourself and always make a positive impression.

———

Speaker of the House Tip O'Neill had serious policy differences with Reagan. Nevertheless, O'Neill described Reagan as "an exceptionally congenial and charming man..., a terrific storyteller,...witty, and he's got an excellent sense of humor."[17] In *Man of the House*, O'Neill recalled his first meeting with the new president: "When President-elect Reagan came to my office in November of 1980, we two Irish-American pols got right down to business by swapping stories about the Notre Dame football team. I told Reagan how much I had enjoyed his Knute Rockne movie, and he graciously pointed out that his friend Pat O'Brien was the real star of that film."[18]

O'Neill went on to tell Reagan that despite his "various disagreements in the House," he and the Republican leadership "were always friends after six o'clock and on weekends." "The president-elect seemed to like that formulation, and over the next six years he would often begin our telephone discussions by saying, 'Hello, Tip, is it after six o'clock?'...[E]ven with our many intense political battles, we managed to maintain a pretty good friendship."[19]

There may be people in your world who will not agree with you on the employment of resources, capital expenditures, marketing programs, pay, and bonuses. Do not let a matter of business become a personal thing. You will get more done and enjoy the journey along the way.

———

Ed Meese wrote of Reagan that "humor was part of his personality and contributed to his management style by reducing tension and keeping up morale....He knew that laughter was a tonic for people who were working long and hard on contentious matters."[20]

Reagan routinely joked about his age, once noting "that wage and price controls had continually failed since the time of the Roman emperor Diocletian." He added, "I'm the only one here old enough to remember."[21] On occasion he would say, "I've already lived some twenty years longer than my life expectancy was at birth, and that has been a source of annoyance to a number of people."[22]

At the annual Salute to Congress dinner sponsored by the Washington Press Club Foundation in February 1981, he said: "I know your organization was founded by six Washington newspaperwomen in 1919—seems only yesterday."[23]

Reagan famously used humor to play himself down after his first debate with Walter Mondale in 1984. When some questioned if at seventy-three Reagan was too old to serve another term, Reagan delivered the now-famous line, "I am not going to exploit for political purposes my opponent's youth and inexperience." His fifty-six-year-old opponent joined the audience in laughter.

Reagan enjoyed teasing the press. Once he used a joke to diffuse the tension often felt between the press and a president "under fire" in press conferences. "I've got a news item for you...," he said. "We have a spin-off from our 'Star Wars' research. It's a helmet for me to wear at press conferences. All I do is push a button and it shoots down incoming questions."[24]

Humor is a fabulous way to play yourself down. An appropriate sense of humor shows you do not take yourself too seriously. It invites communication and promotes a more cooperative environment for your team.

In her book *Thanks for the Memories, Mr. President*, Helen Thomas wrote: "Self-deprecation was [Reagan's] stock-in-trade, and his timing skills had been honed for years before a camera—even his comparing himself to Methuselah was funny. He loved to tell stories that amplified his sense of optimism and patriotism....Age and big government were his mainstays for humorous opening lines and a good way to win over audiences."[25]

After his near-fatal shooting, Reagan's spontaneous humor reassured members of his administration, as well as the country. It also proved that his wit was not merely scripted. The day after surgery, Ed Meese, James Baker, and Mike Deaver came to the hospital to see him. The president was propped up in bed, brushing his teeth. "I should have known I wasn't going to avoid a staff meeting," he quipped.[26] When they told him he would be pleased to know that the government was running as usual, he retorted, "What makes you think I'd be happy about that?"[27]

———

Once Reagan invited Mike Deaver's daughter Amanda to Camp David for her birthday and treated her to a private viewing of *Bedtime for Bonzo*, in which Reagan starred.

Mike Deaver was amazed, given that *Bedtime for Bonzo* was "the movie that may be the butt of more jokes and comedy skits than any other film ever made....It's worth saying again: he was a man without artifice."[28]

Can you show an interest in the children of your teammates on "kids' day" at your office? Perhaps you could teach a Junior Achievement class at a neighborhood school, teach a Sunday school class at church, or lead a scout troop. You can be a positive role model for students by showing a genuine interest in them and by sharing a few laughs along with your mentoring. You make a difference in their lives when you show them you are not too busy or "important" to spend time with them.

———

Leaders prove they do not take themselves too seriously when they can laugh at what might be considered "sore subjects." Reagan often joked with the studio crew before radio addresses. Unaware that the microphone was live, Reagan once said, "My fellow Americans, I am pleased to announce I have just signed legislation which outlaws Russia forever. We begin bombing in five minutes."

During the Iran-Contra investigation in 1987, Reagan referred to a string of presidential "sore subjects" in this light-hearted moment at a press dinner: "With the Iran thing occupying everyone's attention, I was thinking: Do you remember the flap when I said, 'We begin bombing in five minutes'? Remember when I fell asleep during my audience with the pope? Remember Bitburg? Boy, those were the good old days. I have to admit we considered making one final shipment to Iran, but no one could figure out how to get [ABC News correspondent] Sam Donaldson in a crate."[29]

Reagan even liked to tell jokes to Gorbachev. One of his favorites was about an American and a Russian arguing over their countries' merits. The American says, "Look, in my country I can walk into the Oval Office, I can pound the president's desk and say, 'Mr. President, I don't like the way you're running our country!'" The Russian replies, "I can do that, too." "You can?" says the American. "Yes," says the Russian, "I can march into the general secretary's office, I can pound on his desk and say, 'Mr. General Secretary, I don't like the way President Reagan's running his country!'" Gorbachev laughed.[30]

Can you develop the ability to poke fun at yourself? Develop a standard stick that puts you down, plays you down, pokes fun at your department or profession. Do this in a tasteful, professional way. You will diffuse tension and disarm hostility, and others will rush to support you.

We may never be as quick-witted as Reagan, but we can learn to see the world through a lighter lens. We can take ourselves less seriously. We can learn to play ourselves down. As we do, we will endear ourselves to others, win over opposition, and earn others' respect. We will rally our organization to peak performance and improve our organization in every area, from morale to the bottom line.

Leadership Principle 8

"There is no limit to what a man can do or where he can go if he doesn't mind who gets the credit."
            Sign on Ronald Reagan's desk in the Oval Office

Validate Their Ideas

David Gergen, advisor to four presidents and White House communications director from 1981 to 1983, recalled that the diverse team Ronald Reagan assembled in 1981 was crucial to the success of his first term as president. Many of the advisors Reagan brought to the White House had known him for years. The president was aware that to be successful in Washington, he also needed people who were experienced in government on the national level and knew the intricacies of political life in the Capitol.[1] The ability of conservatives and moderates to work together to further the common goals of the new administration was a hallmark of the Reagan White House.

In 1980 Reagan added George H. W. Bush to the presidential ticket. Together they had won 85 percent of the primary vote. Reagan

136

recognized that Bush would help unify the party and broaden support for the ticket. He also valued the federal government and foreign affairs experience Bush would bring.[2]

"The coalition government [conservatives and moderates] that [Reagan] created at the White House in his early years was one of the strongest teams in the past forty years," wrote Gergen in *Eyewitness to Power*. "As a man who liked to delegate, Reagan needed an effective group around him....Privately, I admired Reagan for welcoming so many moderates aboard."[3]

Ronald Reagan was a visionary who led from high ideals and a practical leader who knew he could not achieve his goals alone. He surrounded himself with capable, creative people who could invent practical solutions to problems and lay out feasible means for achieving the ultimate vision.

An important aspect of leadership is giving credit for ideas and achievements to your team. You boost their confidence, morale, and creativity by validating their ideas, by "letting it be the other person's idea." Even if you think you thought of the idea first, let others have the credit. Let it be their idea.

———

In *My Turn*, Nancy Reagan wrote that

every time her husband met with Mikhail Gorbachev, he brought up religious freedom, particularly "the rights of Jews...to leave the country. On several occasions Ronnie gave Gorbachev a list of people who, in our view, deserved to be allowed to leave. 'Do what you can,' Ronnie would say. 'I'll never mention these names to the press, and I'll never take credit for it if you let them go.' Many of these people were subsequently released."[4]

Former Secretary of State George Shultz said that President Reagan made a point of not "grandstanding:" "He preferred to get something done than to get credit for it."[5]

As an empowering leader, you too can get more done if you allow those you work with to get the credit. It is not your ego that matters. Rather, it is getting the job done by empowering others to use their creativity to find solutions and to take action. Keep yourself in the background and let others have the glory. The success of your teammates is the measure of your own success.

———

Democratic House Speaker Tip O'Neill credited the "strong, capable people around" Reagan with the president's success in getting his legislative agenda passed. Wrote the speaker,

"[T]hey knew where they were going and they knew how to get there." O'Neill vehemently disagreed with the Reagan administration, but they won his respect.[6]

Reagan was a macromanager, a delegator who challenged his team to use their creativity to come up with the details. He provided the context—vision, values, and standards—and expected the staff to work out the content. He wanted them to innovate, create, and develop their own ideas, rather than receive mandates about how to do things from the top, down. He wanted an environment in which the talents of each associate could flourish for the good of the enterprise as a whole.

David Laux, formerly of the National Security Council, said Reagan had a "sense of balance." "While [Reagan] was great at delegating, he knew when to step in and take hold: to make a decision or emphasize a point," he said.[7]

Empowering leaders know that delegating does not mean passing off accountability. Rather, delegating is letting other members of the team exercise responsibility, freeing up the leader's time while bringing a fresh approach and new ideas to the party. As an empowering leader, you will use your own time more efficiently if you reserve your time for tasks that you alone should do. Empower others to contribute to the team effort. If others have the capacity to develop their capability, move tasks off your desk and empower them to take the steps to grow. If others can do something better than you can, or if it is a step in their career growth, let them do it.

———

Former Secretary of the Treasury Donald Regan was not comfortable at first with President Reagan's management style. He expected to receive detailed instructions from the president. Eventually he understood that from Reagan's perspective, he *had* received instructions.

"In 1981 I had not yet begun to understand that this was the way Ronald Reagan did business," Regan wrote, "that his public persona *was* his real persona. For a while I struggled against a certain anxiety that this method of running the world's greatest economy might wreck the new Presidency. Happily, I was wrong. In fact Reagan's openness created an atmosphere of confidence and political dynamism that produced the longest period of recovery and the highest levels of employment in the history of the United States....

"After a short time I realized that there was no good reason why the President should call his Secretary of the Treasury into his presence and tell him confidentially that he had meant what he said about federal spending and fiscal and monetary policy in his campaign speeches and his other public utterances....

"My basic position was simple. Ronald Reagan had been elected by the American people to carry out the ideas and programs he had discussed in his campaign. My job was to identify these promises and do my best to translate them into policy and programs."[8]

Because Reagan's philosophy was so well-defined, it was easy for his administration to implement it in policy. "For example," wrote former White House Counsel Peter Wallison, "since there was no question that Reagan wanted to reduce the role of government in the economy, it was not necessary for him to press his administration for specific deregulatory programs; these welled up from the cabinet departments as they sought to respond to Reagan's well-known overall objectives."[9]

For your team to achieve its full potential in working toward common goals, it is crucial for the objective to be clearly defined. Reagan understood his role as an empowering leader to be defining the goal and then unleashing his team to use their expertise and creativity to work out the details. An empowering leader knows it is impossible to personally "run" every aspect of a large enterprise. It is counterproductive to inhibit your team's ability to use their own skills and talents. Maximize your team's productivity by defining the goal and then encouraging them to be proactive in creating solutions.

In your organization you have five levels of authority and initiative: 1) do and report routinely, 2) do and report immediately, 3) recommend and do, 4) ask what to do, 5) wait to be told. You empower your team when you create an environment in which team members can "move up a rung," from level 5 to level 4, etc. As they grow in skill and capacity for responsibility, your enterprise becomes more efficient.

Managers resist delegation for many reasons. They feel they can do everything better themselves, they do not trust their team members, they fear "mis-takes," they are not inclined to develop team members' potential, or they do not want to let go of the level of control they are used to having. Overcoming these barriers is well worth the effort. Empowering leaders find they have a more efficient and powerful team, and their team members find pride and satisfaction in their own personal growth and their more effective contribution to the total effort.

In his autobiography, Reagan laid out his management style:

"I had to select the best people I could find for my administration—people whom I could rely on and trust....

"Then, I had to set policies and goals I wanted these people to accomplish....

"I don't believe a chief executive should supervise every detail of what goes on in his organization. The chief executive should set broad policy and general ground rules, tell people what he or she wants them to do, then let them do it; he should make himself (or *her*self) available, so that the members of his team can come to him if there is a problem. If there is, you can work on it together and, if necessary, fine-tune the policies. But I don't think a chief executive should peer constantly over the shoulders of the people who are in charge of a project and tell them every few minutes what to do.

"I think that's the cornerstone of good management....As long as they are doing what you have in mind, don't interfere, but if somebody drops the ball, intervene and make a change."[10]

Margaret Thatcher said "[i]t was easy for lesser men to underrate Ronald Reagan....His style of work and decision-making was apparently detached and broad-brush....He laid down clear general directions for his Administration, and expected his subordinates to carry them out at the level of detail."[11]

Delegating—letting go, giving up control—is one of the chief challenges managers face. They often hang on too long to things they should put into others' hands. Once you have brought yourself to the point of letting go, the steps to effective delegation are very important. Ronald Reagan seemed to follow these steps intuitively.

First, ensure the context is understood by using the occasion of delegation as one more opportunity to refer to the mission, vision, values, and overall goals of the enterprise. Delegate according to the results to be achieved, including why successful execution is important. Define authority and clarify responsibilities. Second, get a proposed action plan from the assignee. Third, agree on time tables for milestone check-ins and achievement of the goal or completion of the task. Fourth, agree on a reporting system to maximize accountability. Finally, take corrective action when necessary. Don't micromanage now for fear of possibly having to correct later. Instead, help your team develop their skills and capacity for initiative. Don't fear "mis-takes."

In 1977 Reagan upheld the truth that the strength of an organization is its members. At the Fourth Annual Conservative Political Action Conference, he said: "Our party must be based on the kind of leadership that grows and takes its strength from the people. Any organization is in actuality only the lengthened shadow of its members. A political party is a mechanical structure created to further a cause. The cause, not the mechanism, brings and holds the members together."[12]

In Reagan's White House, he actively invited his team to give him their input at any time, on any subject. He encouraged them to think out-of-the-box. He wanted the best people on his team, no matter who they were.

In 1980 Mike Deaver suggested that James Baker, George Bush's former campaign manager, become Reagan's White House chief of staff. Deaver was impressed that Reagan "didn't laugh [him] out of the room." He wrote: "Here I was suggesting a guy for the most important job in the administration who not only worked against us in 1980 but also had been part of the Ford operation in 1976. If there was any Republican who didn't seem to be a Reaganite, it was probably Jimmy Baker.

"Instead of laughing, Reagan looked at

me and asked, 'Do you think he'll do it?'"[13] Reagan did offer Baker the job, and Baker accepted. It was the first time a president-elect had offered such a high-level White House position to the campaign manager of a former opponent.[14]

Reagan's White House demonstrated how you can use delegation as an empowering leader. Ed Meese wrote that the basic ideas of Reagan's economic program "were vintage Reagan," but that "the particular shape that they assumed owed a great deal to the economic advisors on whom he called, both during the campaign and in the White House."[15]

One way Reagan commonly validated others' ideas was to ask rhetorical questions. In his October 28, 1980 debate with Jimmy Carter, he did not say, "America is worse off today...." He invited voters to ask themselves, "Are you better off today than you were four years ago?" David Gergen cited this episode as another instance in which Reagan made his team "work magically together."

"It was Reagan who had demonstrated the power of rhetorical questions through long years of practice," he wrote. "It was [Richard] Wirthlin who had observed him closely and was smart enough to know we should go to that well now. I had the understanding of how then to distill the thought into a question that defined the reality so many Americans were experiencing. Each of us—Reagan, Wirthlin, and I—benefited from the talents of the others. One savors moments like that in politics."[16]

In 1987 Dinesh D'Souza came to the White House as a senior domestic policy analyst. "We were a generation of young conservatives who came to Washington in the 1980s inspired by Reagan and the idea of America that he espoused and embodied," he wrote. "The world was changing, and we wanted to be instruments of that change. Reagan was a septuagenarian with a youthful heart. He hired people like me because he wanted fresh faces and new ideas in the White House. Full of vigor and determination, we rallied to his cause."[17]

This style of management—validating the ideas of others—requires that the leader have confidence in the team. You rely on them and have the advantage and satisfaction of unleashing their creativity. The leader who gets the most done finds ways to leverage and meld the differences and strengths of every member of the team. Some people have a natural interest in product appearance, others in structural integrity; some in new products for current markets, others in new markets for current products. By validating the ideas of others, the empowering leader builds a stronger organization, not just a better product.

———

Empowering leaders make the most of the strengths of their team members by using their ideas. They encourage them to use their creativity to invent and innovate new approaches to processes and find solutions to troubling problems. They give credit to others and reward effort with praise, even before success is achieved. Empowering leaders validate their team and multiply their productivity and effectiveness.

Empowering leaders know that the only unique advantage of their organization does not come from machines, location, products, or dealers, as important as these may be. Empowering leaders know deeply that their unique advantage is derived from the combined creativity and innovative potential of their team. Competitors across the country and around the world have access to the same technology, the same or similar suppliers, and all the resources that go into the mix that makes up a firm. The only resource to which competitors do not have access is your people. In fully tapping and harnessing the ideas of your team, the organization becomes a sustainable learning environment and experiences constant improvement.

Leadership Principle 9

In his landmark speech of October 27, 1964, Reagan mentioned juvenile delinquency centers that cost taxpayers $4,700 per inmate per year. He exclaimed, "We can send them to Harvard for $2,700!"

Ronald Reagan[1]

Dramatize Your Ideas

When Ronald Reagan was governor of California, he proudly announced that the state government was saving hundreds of millions of dollars by upgrading efficiency though business-savvy practices. "I'd...get a glassy stare and polite applause," he wrote. Reagan realized that ordinary people had a hard time visualizing hundreds of millions of dollars, "or even one million for that matter."

Then he mentioned that $200,000 had been saved by sending automobile registration renewal notices earlier than necessary because postal rates were about to increase. "The audience came to their feet with a roar of approval. Two hundred thousand dollars they could visualize. Two hundred million, they couldn't."[2]

Reagan learned from this experience in California that while facts and figures have true meaning, their real-world implications can be difficult to grasp. In an Oval Office address to the nation on February 5, 1981, Reagan made the case for his anti-inflation economic policy by holding up a dollar bill and some coins.

"Here is a dollar such as you earned, spent, or saved in 1960," he said. "And here is a quarter, a dime, and a penny—thirty-six cents. That's what this 1960 dollar is worth today. And if the present world inflation rate should continue three more years, that dollar of 1960 will be worth a quarter. What [incentive] is there to save?"[3]

During the 1984 campaign, Reagan illustrated the financial impact of his opponent's budget and tax plan by comparing it with a home mortgage: "If [Walter Mondale] is to keep all the promises he's made..., he will have to raise taxes by the equivalent of $1,890 per household. That's more than $150 a month. It's like having a second mortgage. And after the Mondale Mortgage we're sure to see more than a few foreclosures!"[4]

Empowering leaders not only have vision and high ideals, they spark the imaginations of their listeners by dramatizing their ideas. Merely stating an idea—laying out the facts—is not enough. When we talk about and sell our ideas, we must ensure that our ideas penetrate the preoccupation of the listeners and find a place of importance in their minds.

Leaders do this by speaking with vivid pictorial detail. They speak dramatically, often by combining something "new" with something familiar to the audience. When your audience can visualize what you are saying, they understand your ideas. Understanding is the first step to conviction, and conviction is required for action.

——

"Not since Lincoln, or Winston Churchill in Britain, has there been a president who has so understood the power of words to uplift and inspire," Lady Margaret Thatcher said of Ronald Reagan.[5] Reagan loved to tell stories and was a dynamic dramatic speaker.

Ronald Reagan began to hone his talent as a young man in radio and continued to develop it throughout his career. He believed in the power of the spoken word to vividly communicate ideas. Just out of college, Reagan wanted to be a radio sports announcer. He appreciated the immediacy of the spoken word and came to admire Franklin Roosevelt and his Fireside Chats. Radio was "theater of the mind.

It forced you to use your imagination," Reagan said.[6]

During a hiring interview, the director of WOC in Davenport, Iowa asked Reagan to describe a football game "and make me *see* it as if I was home listening to the radio."

Reagan extemporaneously "replayed" the fourth quarter of one of his own college football games: *"Here we are in the fourth quarter with Western State University leading Eureka College six to nothing....Long blue shadows are settling over the field and a chill wind is blowing in through the end of the stadium...."* He was hired on the spot.[7]

"Once I was on the air," Reagan wrote of his first week at WOC, "I tried to make the most of my opportunity and chose phrases and adjectives I hoped would give listeners visual images that would make them think they were in the stadium, and I laced my descriptions with background about the players and teams that I hoped would demonstrate that I knew what I was talking about."[8]

When he decided to run for president, Reagan explained how he felt with a story: "...I remember in the movie *Santa Fe Trail*, I played George Custer as a young lieutenant. The dying captain said to me, 'You have got to take over.' And my line was 'I can't, I can't.' And the captain said, 'You must, it's your duty.' That's the way I feel about this, it's my duty."[9]

When Reagan was governor of California, a young man suggested that Reagan might seem more relevant to young people if he rode a motorcycle. Reagan replied that he would have to stick with horseback riding, explaining, "You see, there is the matter of security. When I go [any place], I'm one of a group. We might look like Hell's Angels with all of us out there on motorcycles.'"[10]

Empowering leaders lead the audience with images that reinforce their vision and the ideas they are endeavoring to impart. "A picture is worth a thousand words." Stories, images, and vivid examples communicate your ideas and ideals. Abstract concepts fail to create pictures in the mind; attractive images pull us forward and motivate us to action.

———

The owner of WOC, B. J. Palmer, was a master of advertising. He taught his announcers to "smile your voice," to be "conversational and personal," and to "use showmanship."[11] Following Palmer's advice, young Reagan practiced and eventually developed that pleasant and persuasive voice for which he became famous. His perseverance, euphonious voice, and talent for description made the nobody from

Dixon a local celebrity. As president of the United States, he conveyed to a new generation the world over that same confidence and optimism which FDR had inspired in him fifty years before.

Your voice is the instrument on which you play the symphony of your life. Take the time to develop it. Be conscious of your pacing and modulation. You may have limited control over the pitch of your voice; but you can learn to speak from your diaphragm, control your pacing, and decide how and when to show emphasis.

———

Before Reagan traveled across the country for General Electric, giving speeches illustrating what he believed makes America great, he presented the same themes through his roles as an actor, first on film and later on television.

Reagan liked to play roles which highlighted what was good about America and her history. In 1947 he told gossip columnist Louella Parsons that he preferred "Western or outdoor pictures..., preferably with a historical flavor."[12] He was also fond of "athletic pictures, football or baseball or whatever, to *show* the principles America lives by; the pioneer spirit, the sportsmanship, the health and courage" of

Americans.[13]

Give careful thought to the images you permit in your workplace. They dramatize who you are. Take stock of the pictures, posters, slogans, and books your team members display. These images tell a story about who you are as an organization. They are part of your organization's persona, a mosaic of your values. Do not abdicate responsibility for what can be seen on screensavers, lockers, tool boxes, and bulletin boards. Apply the same standard litmus test of Ronald Reagan to ensure that these images portray a pioneer spirit, good sportsmanship, health, and courage.

———

The "salesman" never left Reagan. As president, he once dropped in on his campaign advisors and said, "Since you're the ones who are selling the soap, I thought you'd like to see the bar." "The admen got a kick out of it," wrote biographer Lou Cannon. "They liked working for a president who had enough understanding of their work to think of himself as a product."[14]

Regardless of your title, a part of your job is sales. You must be good at personal public relations packaging and selling yourself. Take responsibility for the way you are introduced, packaged, and presented. As an empowering leader, do not rely completely on others to do the packaging for you. Judgments we make about each other are based on what we say, how we say it, what we do, how we do it, and how we look.

Be attentive to the words you choose. Words are symbols to which we have culturally agreed to assign meaning. Since cultures change, so do the meanings of words. Be aware of the way you emphasize or de-emphasize certain words through your pacing and modulation. We can use cues in our voices to add nuance to the words we say and to make their meaning more precise.

Showing up on time, saying hello, rolling our eyes, crossing our arms, and opening the door for others are examples of things we do that convey meaning about our values. Walking briskly, sitting and standing up straight, and how we use our head and hands when we talk communicate our zeal and excitement or our passive lethargy. Our personal appearance, dress, grooming, and how we carry ourselves say a lot about how we think of others, ourselves, our job, and our position. People notice! Be your own best advertisement.

———

Reagan's 1981 inauguration was the first

in history to take place on the West Front of the Capitol. He wanted to illustrate the points he would make in the speech by referring to the monuments in Washington. "Standing here," he said, "one faces a magnificent vista, opening up on this city's special beauty and history. At the end of this open mall are those shrines to the giants on whose shoulders we stand."[15]

Take charge of staging in the room where you give presentations. Be conscious of the way you set up your surroundings. Ensure that you have the props you want and need to make your point and dramatize your ideas.

Reagan's ability to make an audience "see" served him well as president. The empowering leader uses this same ability to help the team see the possible and dramatize the importance, the urgency of the moment, the task at hand.

During the 1984 Olympics, Reagan used Olympic imagery to illustrate what he thought was great about America. Author Paul Erickson wrote in *Reagan Speaks*: "With the audience cheering, 'U.S.A.! U.S.A.! U.S.A.!' President Reagan found in his Olympic imagery one of his favorite rhetorical motifs, the flame of freedom and hope that burns in the hearths of Iowa and that throws light on Berlin."

"In Richardson, Texas," said Reagan, "[the torch] was carried by a 14-year-old boy in a special wheelchair. In West Virginia the runner came across a line of deaf children and let each one pass the torch for a few feet, and at the end these youngsters' hands talked excitedly in their sign language. Crowds spontaneously began singing 'America the Beautiful' or 'The Battle Hymn of the Republic.'

"Then in San Francisco a Vietnamese immigrant, his little son held on his shoulders, dodged photographers and policemen to cheer a 19-year-old black man pushing an 88-year-old white woman in a wheelchair as she carried the torch....My friends, that's America."[16]

Do not be afraid to step up and use dramatic metaphors to illustrate your ideals, mission, and vision. Tie your message, your campaign, your theme for the month or Monday meeting to a "brand"—an event—that is bigger than your firm. Identify values and images which are vivid in the public's mind. Draw parallels between these idealized images/events and your mission, vision, and values, as Reagan did with the Olympics.

———

During a meeting on economic policy, President Reagan noted the problem with not having a visionary imagination: "You know, back in the twenties I think they did a report for

Herbert Hoover about what the future economy would be like. And they included all their projections on industries and restaurants and steel, everything. But you know what they left out? They left out radio! They left out the fantastic rise of the media, which transformed the commercial marketplace. And those were economists talking about the future!

"And now they make their projections, and they leave out high tech...."[17]   An empowering leader has vision that extends beyond the conventional thinking that limits the vistas the organization can scale, and then describes to others where they can travel together as a team. This vision leads your organization to continuously improve products and services and to discover new products and new markets for existing products. Use upbeat, descriptive language to get your vision across. Spark your team's imagination, and they will be motivated to create the breakthroughs needed to fulfill the mission and achieve the vision.

———

Reagan's flair for dramatization made a lasting impression on others. At the 1980 convention Reagan asked Gerald Ford if he and Nancy might drop by the Fords' hotel room. When Reagan arrived, he immediately handed the former president an Indian peace pipe, signifying that he wanted to put their differences behind them. Ford was touched by this gesture and kept the peace pipe in his office throughout his retirement.[18]

At the 1985 Geneva conference, Reagan arrived at the Villa Fleur d'Eau before Gorbachev. When Gorbachev's car drove up to the château in the bitter cold of a Swiss winter, Reagan came bounding down the stairs to meet him without topcoat or hat. Gorbachev emerged swathed in a gigantic coat, scarf, and hat. Reagan offered Gorbachev his arm as they climbed the stairs.

Sergei Tarasenko, a prominent member of the Soviet press, later said that his country "started with the wrong move."[19] Ken Adelman, former deputy U.S. representative to the United Nations, said that in the eyes of the press, Reagan "personified a vigorous and forward-looking America," while Gorbachev "looked as cold and lumbering as the country he ruled."[20] How the two men appeared in those photographs affected how people around the world perceived the nations they represented.

Former presidential chief of staff Kenneth Duberstein recalled an incident from the 1987 Washington, D.C. summit during which Reagan and Gorbachev signed the INF Treaty. The two leaders had a private meeting in the Oval Office.

Reagan picked up a baseball, tossed it up in the air a couple of times, and asked Gorbachev, "[D]o you want to play ball, or do you want to be stuck in ideological differences[?]" Gorbachev reportedly replied, "Let's play ball."[21]

In your position as an empowering leader, be aware of the impact of images on those with whom you interact. Whenever possible, dramatize your message. Remember that your personal appearance and demeanor affect the way others think of you and consequently how they view your ideas. People size each other up within the first couple minutes. A good first impression is vital to your success in leading, communicating, and working with others, and winning the day.

———

Ronald Reagan was a powerful storyteller. He preferred to get his point across dramatically whenever possible. At Notre Dame's commencement in 1981, Reagan explained the genesis of "win one for the Gipper," making it a universal challenge for team success.

"'Win one for the Gipper,'" he said, "has become a line usually spoken now in a humorous vein....But let's look at the real significance of his story. Rockne could have used it any time just to win a game. But eight years would go by following the death of George Gipp before Rock ever revealed Gipp's deathbed wish.

"Then he told the story at half time to one of the only teams he'd ever coached that was torn by dissension, jealousy, and factionalism. The seniors on that team were about to close out their football careers without ever learning or experiencing some of the real values the game has to impart.

"None of them had ever known George Gipp. They were children when he played for Notre Dame. Yet it was to this team that Rockne told the story and so inspired them that they rose above their personal animosities. They joined together in a common cause and attained the unattainable.

"We were told of one line spoken by a player during that game that we were afraid to put in the picture. The man who carried the ball over for the winning touchdown was injured on the play. We were told that as he was lifted on the stretcher and taken off the field he was heard to say, 'That's the last one I can get for you, Gipper.'

"Yes, it was only a game and it might seem somewhat maudlin, but is there anything wrong with young men having the experience of feeling something so deeply that they can give so completely of themselves? There will come times in the lives of all of us when we'll be faced with causes bigger than ourselves and they won't be on a playing field."[22]

Yes, it may sound maudlin, but if you do not find a way to enroll the heart of your team, you let them down. They want a cause to champion, to give themselves to. When they give themselves to your cause, you have a competitive advantage that money alone cannot buy.

———

In his farewell address in January 1989, Reagan told this amazing story, which vividly dramatized his ideals, his vision as a leader, and his concept of America:

"I've been reflecting on what the past eight years have meant and mean. And the image that comes to mind like a refrain is a nautical one—a small story about a big ship, and a refugee, and a sailor. It was back in the early eighties, at the height of the boat people. And the sailor was hard at work on the carrier *Midway*, which was patrolling the South China Sea. The sailor, like most American servicemen, was young, smart, and fiercely observant. The crew spied on the horizon a leaky little boat.

And crammed inside were refugees from Indochina hoping to get to America. The *Midway* sent a small launch to bring them to the ship and safety. As the refugees made their way through the choppy seas, one spied the sailor on deck and stood up and called out to him. He yelled, 'Hello, American sailor. Hello, freedom man.'

"A small moment with a big meaning, a moment the sailor, who wrote it in a letter, couldn't get out of his mind. And when I saw it, neither could I. Because that's what it was to be an American in the 1980s. We stood, again, for freedom. I know we always have, but in the past few years the world again, and in a way, we ourselves—rediscovered it."[23]

Ronald Reagan knew the importance of getting his ideas across to an audience. As an empowering leader, you can do the same by inventing dramatic ways of describing your ideas so they fire up the imaginations and enthusiasm of your team. "An example is better than a sermon," Reagan said.[24] Get your team inspired by your mission, and you will see breakthroughs in motivation, morale, and productivity.

Leadership Principle 10

"Mr. Gorbachev, tear down this wall!"
Ronald Reagan at the Brandenburg Gate[1]

Stimulate Competition

"Yes, change your world," Ronald Reagan challenged his audience in a less-commonly quoted section of his 1983 "Evil Empire" speech. "One of our Founding Fathers, Thomas Paine, said, 'We have it within our power to begin the world over again.' We can do it...."[2]

What a challenge! You may be just as challenged in your own department or company to change your world. Our world is changing fast, and yesterday's records are today's norm. If you do not create a team that responds to the challenge of increased competition, you will be replaced. Keep score, trend charts, make a game out of the challenge you throw down to your team to ensure you make continuous improvement the norm. As an empowering leader, you set the stage for improvement in your world by stimulating competition among your associates.

Throwing down a challenge raises expectations and brings out the best in yourself and in others. Money alone does not bring good people together, nor does it hold them together. Exciting ideas do! The chance to prove their worth and the opportunity to win creates and maintains an unbeatable team. Empowering leaders know they can help people discover their untapped potential by increasing the challenge, not the workload. The difference between the two is often the perspective of your team.

———

Ronald Reagan focused on priorities. He did not allow himself to be distracted by peripheral things. Instead of getting lost in petty details, he set his sights on the big picture.[3] "Reagan was more like Demosthenes [than Ciccro]," wrote Dinesh D'Souza; "he deployed his famous skills not to display his own eloquence but to generate support for his ideas."[4] He used his oratory to win people over to his point of view and then challenged them to do something about it. He urged them, for instance, not just to agree with him but to register their support with their representatives in Congress.[5] He challenged us to challenge them.

Presidential advisor David Gergen wrote that Reagan effectively used the differences among his staff to make the whole team stronger: "A half century earlier, FDR frequently pitted his aides against each other in drawing up policies and speeches. The tensions between them set off sparks, making his White House more creative. Whether Reagan was consciously copying the Roosevelt model, I'm not sure, but the system he set up had much the same effect....[T]he tensions Reagan introduced within his team had at least one positive result: they turned his senior staff into toughened professionals ready to take on the outside world."[6]

Constructive debates and disagreements among your team are healthy. If you have two people who agree on everything, you have one too many people. An environment of positive brainstorming of different approaches and angles allows people to think through new ideas and build on each other's strengths. Great leaders bring out the best in those who work for and with them by encouraging and validating their creativity. When all members of an organization contribute their individual strengths and diversity to a project, the opportunity for success increases exponentially.

In his historic speech at the Brandenburg Gate, West Berlin, Reagan boldly challenged Gorbachev to take further steps in his emerging policy of *glasnost* (openness to critical discussion of political and social issues within the USSR). He dared to challenge Gorbachev to do something momentous that most people thought was impossible:

"And now the Soviets themselves may, in a limited way, be coming to understand the importance of freedom....

"Are these the beginnings of profound changes in the Soviet state? Or are they token gestures, intended to raise false hopes in the West, or to strengthen the Soviet system without changing it? We welcome change and openness; for we believe that freedom and security go together, that the advance of human liberty can only strengthen the cause of world peace. There is one sign the Soviets can make that would be unmistakable, that would advance dramatically the cause of freedom and peace.

"General Secretary Gorbachev, if you seek peace, if you seek prosperity for the Soviet Union and Eastern Europe, if you seek liberalization: Come here to this gate! Mr. Gorbachev, open this gate! Mr. Gorbachev, tear down this wall!"[7]

Reagan's challenge was not empty

rhetoric. The freedom he envisioned was a reality a mere two and a half years later. On November 9, 1989 the government of East Germany ended restrictions on travel between the two sectors of Berlin. The following year free elections were held in East Germany, resulting in non-Communist control of the government. By the end of 1990, Germany was reunified.

Nineteen eighty-nine was a similarly fascinating year in the Soviet Union. Elections were held which resulted in the defeat of many top Communist party officials. Over the next couple of years, change was rapid. Non-Communist political parties were permitted. The Baltic republics declared independence. In 1990 all fifteen republics of the Soviet Union declared that laws passed by their own legislatures took precedence over those of the central government.

Following a failed coup in August 1991, Gorbachev resigned as head of the Communist party but retained the office of president of the USSR. The Supreme Soviet suspended all Communist party activities indefinitely. More republics declared independence. On December 8, 1991, Boris Yeltsin and the presidents of Byelorussia and Ukraine announced that they had formed a new confederation, the Commonwealth of Independent States. On

Christmas Day an amazed world watched Gorbachev's televised resignation as president of the Soviet Union. The USSR had ceased to exist.

By the end of what some call "the Reagan decade," Reagan's challenge had been met, and the Cold War was over.

Reagan wanted to bring the best out of people by challenging them. He was undaunted by the status quo and believed that anyone—everyone—could change for the better. He dared to hope and work for a change in the Communist world that someday would transform rivals into allies. He not only challenged the West to stand firm against further Communist expansion, he challenged the Soviet Union to liberalize. The results were stunning.

What walls, what old paradigms, must you challenge your team to break down or break through? They may seem daunting, but compared with the Soviet status quo, not so impossible! Be courageous, throw down the challenge, persist. You and your team can win, and your world can be permanently changed for the better.

———

An empowering leader knows that despite success, there is always something new to be accomplished. In the years following his presidency, Ronald Reagan never ceased to lay down a challenge to Americans. In his address to the 1992 Republican National Convention, he said: "My fellow citizens..., I have always believed in you and in what you could accomplish for yourselves and for others.

"And whatever else history may say about me when I'm gone, I hope it will record that I appealed to your best hopes, not your worst fears; to your confidence rather than your doubts. My dream is that you will travel the road ahead with liberty's lamp guiding your steps and opportunity's arm steadying your way....

"May all of you as Americans never forget your heroic origins, never fail to seek Divine guidance, and never lose your natural, God-given optimism."[8]

You have unrealized goals that can stretch you and every member of your team to new heights. When you realize these goals, you will leave your team members with a greater sense of who they truly are, of their greatness and potential, and even awaken them to their destiny. Whatever your goals—whether expanding and updating products, enlarging clientele, increasing efficiency or customer satisfaction, and outpacing the competition— lead your team with a challenge that appeals to their skills, talents, experience, and creativity.

Dare to dream, and change your corner of the world.

Leadership Principle 11

"If you want to know which way to go in the future, you have to know which path you took in the past and where you stepped in a gopher hole along the way."

Ronald Reagan[1]

When You Blow It, Show It

The White House switchboard can reach anyone, any time, anywhere in the world. Ronald Reagan once asked to speak with a Democratic congressman, not knowing the congressman was currently in Australia, where it was three o'clock in the morning. As soon as Reagan realized the congressman was not in the U.S., he apologized, saying, "You know, it's not really me. It's an impostor. I'm sure the real president will call you back at a decent hour."[2]

Everyone makes mistakes. There is a subtle paradox in a style of leadership which admits fallibility. When empowering leaders make mistakes, they admit them quickly and emphatically. It takes real confidence and courage to admit your mistakes.

Aiming for "perfection" paralyzes your ability to innovate because there is no room for error. The road to improvement, to excellence, is paved with missed attempts: "mis-takes." When you aim for excellence rather than perfection, you allow yourself to discover new and better ways of doing things. If you take no risks, you may make no "mis-takes," but you will not have any breakthroughs, either.

When your environment does not allow for error of any kind, your team will be reluctant to take risks. They will become masterful at cover-up. They will play it safe, blame others, keep their heads down, and stick their fingers in the air to test the direction of the wind. A culture that takes no risks, no chances, is a culture in which little improvement occurs, because improvement of any kind is accompanied by risk. An empowering leader creates a team that makes positive use of risk—a team that instead of avoiding risk, falls in love with risk. Such teams and organizations set records and achieve what to others seems impossible.

———

Mike Deaver wrote that Ronald Reagan was not afraid to take risks in the cause of his principles: "Reagan would say time and time again that if given a choice between big deficits and winning the Cold War, he'd take the latter every time. I always marveled at his confidence when he said, 'I'll take full responsibility for this gamble.'"[3]

The vast majority of people are risk-averse, so the empowering leader must work continuously at crafting a culture that rewards risk and eliminates reprisal for failures which result from risk. When leaders make mistakes and admit them, those around them become willing to take responsibility for their mistakes. This open, transparent environment helps to create an empowered team and strengthens self-esteem.

———

A little story from the Geneva conference in 1985 says a lot about Reagan's character. He was supposed to feed the goldfish belonging to the children who normally lived at Maison de Saussure, the private château where he and Nancy were staying during the summit. After a long day of negotiations with Gorbachev, Reagan returned to his room to find one of the goldfish dead. He didn't know why it had died; but "[w]hatever the reason," he wrote, "it had died on my watch and I felt responsible."[4]

Reagan had a staff member take the fish to a pet store and buy two matching replacements. He then wrote the children a letter explaining what had happened. He did not think an apology for the death of a child's goldfish was too insignificant for the president's concern. A leader who is in tune with small things is in good shape to handle big ones.

The ability to admit mistakes and learn from them is developed gradually. Practice admitting small mistakes, and you will find it easier to take responsibility when something really big happens. Developing the ability to take responsibility for small errors, instead of covering them up, will result in the humility and strength of character necessary to lead your team through challenging times.

———

Reagan recorded hundreds of radio commentaries in the 1970s. His producer, Harry O'Connor, was impressed that Reagan never blamed his mistakes on others. If he made a mistake while reading a script, he would say, "Well, I messed up again," not, "Darn those secretaries."[5]

Dinesh D'Souza wrote that Reagan could identify with the average person, the average leader: "Sure, he made mistakes, but that showed he was normal."[6] Reagan was able to lead effectively during the tough times of his presidency, such as the Iran-Contra affair, because he habitually took responsibility for his mistakes. He admitted errors and was honest about identifying areas where he needed to do things differently.

Those who worked with Reagan testified that they rarely saw him angry. That does not mean Reagan didn't have a temper. He had learned to control it, making his own feelings subservient to doing what was right in any given situation. Peter Hannaford wrote that Reagan "had a high boiling point."[7] "I would see Mount Reagan blow only three or four times during my nearly thirty years knowing the man," wrote Mike Deaver.[8] When Mount Reagan blew, Reagan admitted it and apologized.

One notable time was during his first political campaign in 1966. He was accused of being racist. The accusation made him very angry because he knew about prejudice first-hand as the son of an Irish Catholic. Furthermore, some of his and his brother's best childhood friends were black. He had been raised to believe that racism was deeply wrong.

Another time he reacted angrily to an ad he felt was questioning his integrity. The ad particularly hurt him because a close friend was involved with its production. "Reagan knew he had blown it and said as much behind closed doors," said Deaver.[9]

After events like these, Deaver said that Reagan would be most angry with himself for having "lost control." Once "Mount Reagan erupted during a meeting with one of the academic senates from the University of California system. 'Oh, my gosh,' he kept saying. 'That was wrong. I shouldn't have done that.'

"Anger was one thing; enmity was another. And I don't think Ronald Reagan disliked anybody."[10]

These instances show that Reagan had a fiery temper. That his closest associates rarely saw him "lose it" testifies to Reagan's success in overcoming his temper. On those rare occasions when he made the mistake of losing his temper, he quickly admitted it, apologized, and moved on.

When leaders lose their temper, they lose the respect of their team. Your team will respect you for keeping your cool under trying circumstances, and they will respect you even more when you take responsibility and apologize for your mistakes.

———

As governor, Reagan initially told reporters that the budget for the University of California system would not be cut. He later changed his mind. He did not make excuses or pretend he had been initially misunderstood. He simply told reporters, "I goofed."[11]

Ronald Reagan did not let vanity get in the way of taking risks and admitting mistakes. Instead, he often used a little humor as he made an admission. In *The Reagan Wit*, author Bill Adler commented that "[a] person can be funny in many instances while lacking wit or a sense of humor. What gives a person these qualities is the ability to cast laughter over oneself, to take pot shots at one's own failings and mistakes, to admit error or defeat with a bit more than a smile. Indeed, it is this capability that inspires leadership."[12]

———

Ronald Reagan's televised speech on the Iran-Contra affair (March 4, 1987) is a good example of an empowering leader taking responsibility for something that happened "on his watch," even if he was not personally involved in every aspect of it. He laid out a plan for correcting the source of the mistake. Here is what he said (emphasis added):

"I've *paid a price for my silence* in terms of your trust and confidence....

"I've studied the [Tower] board's report. Its findings are honest, convincing, and highly critical; and *I accept them*. And tonight I want to share with you my thoughts on these findings and report to you on the actions I'm taking to implement the board's recommendations.

"First, let me say *I take full responsibility* for my own actions and for those of my administration. As angry as I may be about activities undertaken without my knowledge, *I am still accountable* for those activities....And as personally distasteful as I find secret bank accounts and diverted funds—well, as the Navy would say, this happened on my watch."

"...There are reasons why it happened, *but no excuses. It was a mistake....*

"One thing still upsetting me, however, is that no one kept proper records of meetings and decisions. This led to *my failure* to recollect whether I approved an arms shipment before or after the fact. I did approve it; I just can't say specifically when....

"For nearly a week now, I've been studying the board's report. I want the American people to know that this wrenching ordeal of recent months has not been in vain. I endorse every one of the Tower board's recommendations. In fact, I'm going beyond its recommendations so as to put the house in even better order....

"Now, what should happen when you make a mistake is this: *You take your knocks,*

181

you learn your lessons, and then you move on. That's the healthiest way to deal with a problem....You put things in perspective. You pull your energies together. You change. You go forward."[13]

Empowering leaders do not make excuses. Remember the maxim, "Excuses never look good on me!" Empowering leaders explain what happened and how. They unequivocally take responsibility. They identify improvements that need to be made to prevent further mistakes and take steps to implement them. Then they move on.

———

As an empowering leader, build up the trust of your team during times of success. A good relationship with your team, combined with your willingness to take responsibility for your mistakes, will get you through the storms.

The public trust won by Reagan throughout his presidency supported him through Iran-Contra and allowed him to continue to lead effectively throughout the rest of his term. He wrote to his actor friend Charlton Heston that during July 7-8, 1987, when Oliver North was testifying before the joint hearings of the House and Senate,[14] the White House received almost 2,500 phone calls.

Only 83 were "hostile."[15] Despite the scandal, Reagan left office the most popular outgoing president since Eisenhower.

"The Iran-Contra crisis," wrote former White House Counsel Peter Wallison, "essentially ended with the President's speech to the nation on March 4, 1987....At the time, he looked to many observers like a lame-duck president....

"Yet Ronald Reagan came back. In his last years in the White House he succeeded again, this time in achieving the last of the great goals he had set for his presidency: he signed the first arms-reduction agreement ever negotiated with the Soviet Union, and began a process that would end the Cold War—and even the Soviet Union itself—after he had left office.

"Again, one had to ask: How could he have done this? The answer goes back again to the central point of how he governed—not with craft or manipulation, or through the gradual accretion of political power..., but through his ideas and convictions. He believed, and acted on his beliefs; he stayed the course."[16]

In a 1994 tribute to Ronald Reagan, Margaret Thatcher testified to Reagan's honesty: "In a time of politicians, you proved yourself a statesman."[17] You can also be a "statesman" by building up the trust of your team by your honesty and integrity during times of failure as well as of success. Admitting and taking responsibility for mistakes separates empowering leaders from those who merely try to save their own faces at the expense of the mission of the team.

Leadership Principle 12

"...I'd learned a few lessons about negotiating: You're unlikely to ever get all you want; you'll probably get more of what you want if you don't issue ultimatums and leave your adversary room to maneuver; you shouldn't back your adversary into a corner, embarrass him, or humiliate him; and sometimes the easiest way to get some things done is for the top people to do them alone and in private."

Ronald Reagan[1]

Avoid Dogmatic Declarations

Former president of the Screen Actors Guild Charlton Heston knew Reagan when Reagan was president of the SAG. "I found Ronald Reagan to be a very skilled negotiator, not least because he was always good-humored," said Heston. "He would never take a confrontational position; he was not dogmatic. He might disagree, but he'd find a way to leave the other side with a feeling that they were good guys, too, and not the enemy. That is hard to do in such situations."[2]

In his autobiography *In the Arena*, Heston

recounted Reagan's success during the 1960 actors' strike, when Reagan was finishing his final term with the SAG. Heston said he and Reagan understood that "the old Marxist dialectic of the employer as the enemy is painfully out of date. What you want is the common good. For that, you have to find common ground."[3]

Reagan knew that in successful negotiation, both sides have to come out winners. Watching Reagan in action, Heston said: "I began to realize...that grinding the other side down in argument isn't really the best tactic, though a lot of union negotiations are still carried on that way." Reagan, he said, was "patient, persistent, moderate, and above all, good-humored, even at three in the morning, going back into caucus to review the same ground yet again."[4]

In the end, Reagan won what the SAG was bargaining for: The studios would fund pension and medical plans, a new concept at that time, and actors would benefit financially when their movies were rereleased on television. Heston called Reagan's negotiation groundbreaking and "the best contract SAG ever negotiated."[5]

Confrontation is not easy but often necessary. Empowering leaders know that people have differences. It is always best to be honest. With a little thought and creativity, you can find ways to be both honest and diplomatic. Never correct in public. Treat everyone with the professional respect with which you want others to treat you. Don't be "puffed up" supervisors or division managers who let ego or petty differences undermine the ultimate achievement of the mission and vision of your team.

———

"Freedom," President Reagan told students at Moscow State University on May 31, 1988, "is the recognition that no single person, no single authority or government has a monopoly on the truth, but...that every one of us put on this world has been put there for a reason and has something to offer."

President Ronald Reagan was an empowering leader with clear principles who led from his ideals. He had well-defined goals and knew what he wanted to accomplish as a leader. He did not find it necessary to resort to dogmatic declarations.

Instead, Reagan surrounded himself with people with ideas. He listened to them and encouraged them to develop strategies to reach the goals. The mission to be accomplished was set. How to get there was up to his administration to negotiate with all the players:

executive branch departments, Congress, voters who express approval or disapproval at the ballot box, foreign allies, and foreign rivals.

An empowering leader avoids dogmatic declarations, like: "As far as I'm concerned...," "This is the way it is," "That's absurd," "That would never work," "That's the craziest idea I've ever heard," "This is the way we've always done it." Dogmatic declarations make others defensive and close the door to understanding, cooperation, and creativity. Avoid giving orders to try to prove who is boss. If you have to prove who is boss, you are not; and you have proven you are not a leader in the least.

Instead of saying, "Why can't you...," develop the habit of saying, "What if we...?" Instead of, "I hate it when...," try, "Wouldn't it be better if...?" When tempted to declare, "We must do it this way," substitute, "Here's a good idea to consider." An empowering leader says, "What is your opinion?" "What do you think?" "What would you do?" "It seems to me," "It appears," "As far as I can tell," "It looks to me like...," and "Do I understand that...?" This one will stretch you: "I could be wrong; I frequently am."

———

Reagan was aware of the polarizing effect

of dogmatic rhetoric. In his 1977 speech to the Fourth Annual Conservative Political Action Conference, he spoke at length on the subject of dogmatic ideology. In this speech he outlined his vision for the modern conservative movement, which he largely redefined and of which he became the icon. While the speech pertains to a political movement, his perspective is relevant to the success of any endeavor, team, or enterprise (emphasis added):

"Whatever ideology may mean—and it seems to mean a variety of things, depending upon who is using it—it always conjures up in my mind a picture of a *rigid, irrational clinging to abstract theory in the face of reality*....

"I consider this to be the complete opposite to principled conservatism....

"Conservatism is the antithesis of the kind of ideological fanaticism that has brought so much horror and destruction to the world. The common sense and common decency of ordinary men and women, working out their own lives in their own way—this is the heart of American conservatism today. Conservative wisdom and principles are derived from *willingness to learn*, not just from what is going on now, but from what has happened before....

"Whatever the word may have meant in the past, today conservatism means *principles evolving from experience and a belief in change*

189

when necessary, but not just for the sake of change."[6]

Reagan believed that having principles doesn't make a person dogmatic. Rather, dogmatism is being unwilling to listen, to understand the other's point of view, to accept their valuable input, to learn from both the past and the present, and to change when change is warranted.

When people become inflexible, defensive—in a word—dogmatic, they feel threatened by another point of view. Often people are defensive because they are unsure of the strength of their own position. They lack the facts to support their case or have never thought through their position.

We often make dogmatic declarations out of fear, hoping the other person will back down. This is not constructive; it is a court of last resort. Confident empowering leaders never have to resort to the desperate approach. They know what they believe and why and so are free to listen to another's point of view without feeling threatened.

———

"[P]eace is the highest aspiration of the American people," said Reagan in his first inaugural address. "We will negotiate for it, sacrifice for it; we will not surrender for it—now or ever."[7]

Ed Meese commented that "like most successful executives, President Reagan combined both toughness and flexibility."[8] He concentrated on the objective like a navigator who keeps his focus on where the team is going. "But in determining how to reach his goal, he was willing to listen to different points of view, and to try different methods if the original approach didn't work."[9]

Meese wrote that Reagan's combination of toughness and flexibility made him a superb negotiator. He would determine what position he believed was in the interest of those for whom he was negotiating (actors, Californians, Americans). Then he would work toward achieving his goal a little at a time. He was willing to take what he could and come back for more, provided that the overall objective was not compromised in the process. If a compromise would make achieving the final objective impossible, he was willing to walk away from negotiations.[10]

For example, Reagan refused to compromise with Gorbachev on the Strategic Defense Initiative at Reykjavík, even though Gorbachev offered historic, unprecedented concessions on missile reductions. Reagan knew that by offering a massive weapons cutback,

191

Gorbachev wanted to neutralize the most effective bargaining tool the U.S. had: SDI.

Reagan shocked the world by not accepting Gorbachev's deal, but he won in the long run. As former Secretary of State George Shultz pointed out, once the Soviet Union indicated that their weapons were up for negotiation, they had lost ground. "[T]he concessions Gorbachev made at Reykjavík could never, in reality, be taken back," Shultz wrote. "We had seen the Soviets' bottom line."[11]

Know the other person's bottom line without allowing them to see yours. Don't tip your hand and let them find out what is the least offer you will take. They may surprise you by offering more than you expected, or someone may suggest a third way neither of you had thought of. Be willing to compromise on details without surrendering your principles. Work toward your desired outcome with your values intact and you will always come out a winner.

———

Presidential advisor Lyn Nofziger first saw Reagan's flexibility in action when Reagan was running for governor. "Reagan...was a jewel," he wrote. "In only a few instances did he exert the candidate's prerogative and demand that things be done his way."[12]

Former senior domestic policy analyst Dinesh D'Souza attested to these traits of Reagan. "Although Reagan was resolute in principle," he wrote, "he was creative and flexible about putting his ideas into practice. Those who called him an extremist and a dogmatist never understood that he was an intensely practical man....He was patient and willing to compromise; if he could not get 100 percent, he would accept half. Yet he was a superb negotiator who usually got 75 percent; he drove an extremely hard bargain."[13]

Reagan liked to agree with FDR's 1933 comment: "I have no expectations of making a hit every time I come to the bat. What I seek is the highest possible batting average."[14] Empowering leaders like Reagan know they often work with people who have either a different vision or a different idea of how to achieve the vision. They understand the importance of negotiation and hone their ability to reach a win-win outcome that ensures the achievement of the goal.

Avoiding dogmatic declarations is a crucial component in building an environment that fosters innovation and creativity. In this environment you can achieve workable solutions to any challenge. An empowering leader knows that the goal—sales growth, return on investment, market share, reduced costs—

cannot be compromised. Strategies and tactics are negotiable. It is important for all parties to come out winners. Good humor, openness, and flexibility go a long way toward reaching your goals and achieving your vision.

Leadership Principle 13

"You know, in our debate, I got a little angry all those times that he distorted my record. And on one occasion, I was about to say to him very sternly, 'Mr. Mondale, you're taxing my patience.' Then I caught myself. Why should I give him another idea? That's the only tax he hasn't thought of."

Ronald Reagan[1]

Avoid Arguments

In a 1983 speech, Ronald Reagan recalled being confronted by a student spokesperson from the University of California during the 1960s. The student said to him, "Governor, it's impossible for you to understand us....Your generation cannot understand their own sons and daughters. You didn't grow up in an era of computers figuring in seconds what it used to take men years to figure out."

Reagan replied, "Wait a minute. It's true what you said. We didn't grow up, my generation, with those things. We invented them."[2]

An empowering leader knows that all

195

arguments are voluntary. Most arguments end with each side more firmly convinced than before that they are absolutely right. You cannot win an argument. When you hurt other people's pride, they resent you. If you lose the argument, you have lost an argument. If you win an argument, you lose a relationship.

When you argue, you lose the cooperation you hoped you would get by defeating the other person. Your team is less empowered when arguments are employed to build consensus. Lady Margaret Thatcher wrote: "[T]here is one principle of diplomacy which diplomats ought to recognize more often: there is no point in engaging in conflict with a friend when you are not going to win and the cost of losing may be the end of the friendship."[3]

———

Those who worked with Ronald Reagan observed that he "fought policies, not people."[4] He tried to avoid petty conflict and personal clashes. He gave team members the benefit of the doubt whenever possible, firing people when necessary for the good of the whole team, but never because of a merely personal conflict.

As president, Reagan fought hard for his agenda, but he never let the political debate get personal. "Partisan labels didn't work with him," wrote Mike Deaver. "Even if you were against him on policy, you could be his friend after hours."[5] For example, Reagan had good personal relationships with Speaker Tip O'Neill and House Ways and Means Chairman Dan Rostenkowski. "These were political giants with whom Reagan had serious policy differences," said Deaver, "but he wouldn't let that interfere with getting to know a good man. With Reagan, it was cocktails at dusk, pistols at dawn."[6]

Reagan employed this strategy in dealing with Gorbachev. He treated the general secretary of the Soviet Union like a real person who could be befriended, not like an impersonal face of the Soviet bureaucracy. He discovered in return that "Gorbachev could be warm and outgoing in a social setting even though several hours earlier we'd had sharp differences of opinion; maybe there was a little of Tip O'Neill in him. He could tell jokes about himself and even about his country, and I grew to like him more."[7] The personal respect and trust Reagan worked to build between himself and the Soviet leader contributed greatly to improving U.S.-Soviet relations.

To continually improve results you must build relationships with those around you, even and especially those with whom you have sharp differences. Building these relationships will be best achieved if you let your ego give up the need to be right about everything and avoid the petty tendency to argue.

———

Former Attorney General Ed Meese described Reagan as a "tough and decisive leader."[8] Reagan "had a friendly and nonconfrontational manner, but it was coupled with resolve and strength."[9] Commentator David Broder, often a critic of Reagan, said that Reagan had "a kind of personal ease and charm that not only delighted his audiences but disarmed his critics."[10]

You do not have to surrender your determination, give up, or give in to avoid arguments. What you must give up is the insistence that you must always be right, always win. Exchange petty egotism for a quiet resolve and a strength that will win every time.

———

Frederick Dutton, an advisor to California Governor Pat Brown, said that Brown's campaign underestimated Reagan in 1966 and that Reagan had "no harsh edge to him." "People like him, and we didn't understand that."[11] Reagan used his humor to defuse and deflect criticism, and so avoid arguments, while making both his opponent and his audience laugh.

Reagan could respond unpredictably. Once he avoided being drawn into an argument by asking, "How can you say that about a sweet fellow like me?"[12] His "there you go again" to Carter in their 1980 debate made him seem in control of the game. His "ease and charm" in deflecting attacks made him look confident.

Like a judo fighter, Reagan turned his opponents' weaknesses back on them. During the Republican presidential candidates' debate in 1980, John Anderson said he would rather see Democratic Senator Ted Kennedy become president than Ronald Reagan. Instead of belaboring the issue, Reagan merely smiled and asked, "John, would you really find Teddy Kennedy preferable to me?" The audience laughed, and Anderson soon found himself running as an independent.[13]

Reagan used jokes to avoid being drawn into debates no one can really win. In a 1984 press conference, Helen Thomas reported that vice presidential candidate Geraldine Ferraro said that Reagan wasn't a good Christian because his "budget cuts have hurt the poor and the disadvantaged." "Do you think you're a good Christian, and why?" asked Thomas. "Well, Helen," replied Reagan, "the minute I heard she'd made that statement, I turned the other cheek."[14]

Reagan used his talent for good humor to avoid acerbic arguments which are so destructive to winning over opponents. Many leaders have yet to realize the strength they would have by eliminating their "sharp edges." Too many leaders in subtle or not-so-subtle ways rely on raw power to convince others to adopt their point of view. They resort to argument at the slightest provocation, forgetting that they may win the argument at the cost of losing the relationship, the respect of their team, and the achievement of the mission of the enterprise. They win the battle but lose the war.

——

Former White House Counsel Peter Wallison described the president as "polite, cordial, and unassuming to all around him...and although he could speak firmly or sharply on matters he cared about, never in my hearing did he raise his voice in anger to a staff member or a political opponent."[15]

George H. W. Bush said of Reagan: "Watching him up close in the White House, I learned that a president could be adversarial without being mean-spirited, that politics did not have to be partisan, so bitter. You could disagree of course—that's the nature of the game—but you did not have to be personally rough. He was always thoughtful, always courteous."[16]

Whatever strategies successful leaders adopt, the empowering leader's first and foremost rule is to avoid arguments. They use caution in handling opposition and influence others by appealing to their common goal. Above all, they remember that arguments are often harmful and nearly always useless. Try to induce others to accept your ideas without forcing them to admit they were in the wrong. Once again, a little humor and good will soften disagreements and save others' pride. When you find it necessary to disagree, do so agreeably.

Leadership Principle 14

"IT CAN BE DONE"
  Sign on Ronald Reagan's desk in the Oval Office

Begin with Yes, Yes

President Reagan knew that his 1986 tax reform plan could not succeed in Congress without Democratic support. He knew that Democratic leaders like Senator Bill Bradley and Congressmen Dick Gephardt and Dan Rostenkowski would favor tax reform if it would close "loopholes for the rich and simplify the tax code."[1] In *Man of the House*, Speaker Tip O'Neill wrote that he was among those who, like Reagan, thought tax reform was "a fine and necessary idea." He was willing to work with Reagan.[2]

Reagan capitalized on the common ground he found with Democratic leaders, taking into account their perspective and bottom line. He successfully negotiated a compromise which achieved the most important aspects of both their goals. The bill Congress passed and Reagan signed closed the "loopholes," as the

Democrats wanted.

The new law also lowered marginal tax rates for individuals and families and reduced the number of tax brackets to only three, as Reagan wanted. It changed the top marginal rate from 50 percent to 28 percent. When Reagan took office in 1981, the top bracket had been 70 percent. The cumulative tax relief he had been able to achieve during his presidency by working with Congress made a significant difference to taxpayers.[3]

"After the vote," wrote O'Neill, "I was struck by how much could be accomplished when the president and the Speaker, coming from opposing parties but working together, could agree on specific legislation....This was one case where leadership made all the difference."[4]

The first step in persuading and leading people is presenting your plans so you get a "yes" response at the very start. Throughout your presentation, but especially at the beginning, get as many "yes's" as you possibly can. Begin by discussing the points on which you agree. Emphasize that you are striving for the same end. This is another opportunity to refer to your mission, vision, and values: "Of course we both want to keep our commitment to our customers" or "We both want a safe, productive work place." Stress when possible that your only difference is one of method, not of purpose.

Empowering leaders make a point of considering in advance the resistance that others may offer. To win cooperation, take those wants and needs into account when you present your plans. If your perspective is that of engineering, consider what manufacturing wants. If you are from sales, consider what finance wants. If you are from packaging, consider what shipping wants.

———

Reagan was a coalition builder abroad as well as at home. During his historic speech at the Brandenburg Gate in 1987, Reagan said: "[W]e must remember a crucial fact: East and West do not mistrust each other because we are armed; we are armed because we mistrust each other."[5] This was one of the first things he had said to Mikhail Gorbachev at the 1985 Geneva conference. As an empowering leader, Reagan believed that he could begin with "yes" even with the general secretary of the Soviet Union.

In *An American Life*, Reagan wrote: "I believed that if we were ever going to break down the barriers of mistrust that divided our countries, we had to begin by establishing a personal relationship between the leaders of the two most powerful nations on earth."[6]

Reagan believed that sometimes it's easier for leaders to reach an understanding if they talk frankly alone, just the two of them.[7] So, he maneuvered a private meeting with Gorbachev in Geneva and said to him: "Here you and I are, two men in a room, probably the only two men in the world who could bring about World War III. But by the same token, we may be the only two men in the world who could perhaps bring about peace in the world."[8] Gorbachev nodded as he listened to the translator.[9]

Reagan banked on the possibility that he and Gorbachev would find common ground, and it paid off. Reagan was determined that the United States could and would win an arms race. Gorbachev feared the U.S. was economically and technologically capable of making good on that promise. Gorbachev did not want a nuclear war, particularly not one his country would lose. Their common ground was that they must work together for peace, knowing the alternative was not a desirable option for either of them.

———

In the late 1990s someone asked Gorbachev what was the "turning point" that resulted in the end of the Communist Soviet Union. "Oh," he replied, "it was Reykjavík."[10]

When Reagan and Gorbachev met at Reykjavík in 1986, Reagan began with "yes, yes" to work steadily toward future success. He negotiated carefully, building on the relationship he and Gorbachev had begun at Geneva. Although the final Intermediate-range Nuclear Forces (INF) treaty was not realized until a year later, at Reykjavík Reagan obtained crucial concessions from the Soviet Union.

The concessions Gorbachev offered at Reykjavík demonstrated that the U.S. and the Soviet Union "had reached virtual agreement on INF and had set out the parameters of START [Strategic Arms Reduction Talks]." "Some of the critics used to say that your positions were too tough," former Secretary of State George Shultz remembered telling Reagan. "Others used to say that they were unrealistic....But at Reykjavík you smoked the Soviets out and they are stuck with their concessions."[11]

Said Reagan in an interview prior to the conference: "It's the initial phase of the negotiating process laying the groundwork, setting the agenda, establishing areas of agreement as well as disagreement that pays off in the future....Now, if that's true of labor and management negotiations here, you can imagine how relevant it is to Soviet-American bargaining sessions; after all, we have a little more separating us than, say, General Motors and the UAW."[12]

When people are saying "yes," they are moving forward, accepting, with an open attitude. The more "yes's" we can get, the more likely we are to succeed in securing cooperation and support for our ultimate proposal. When they are saying "yes," they are with us; we are aligned. When we get a "no," they have dug their heels in, thinking about why they are right and we are wrong. All forward motion stops. Building a relationship of respect and trust is crucial in getting others to be willing to work with us. When you demonstrate consideration of their perspective and requirements, they are more likely to want to find common ground with you.

————

"I am a convinced opponent of a situation where there is a winner and a loser in our meeting," said Gorbachev at Reykjavík. "We must both be winners."[13]

Reagan tried to convince Gorbachev that the United States would share with Russia the same SDI technology that would protect the U.S. and its allies from ballistic missile attacks. Gorbachev did not trust Reagan, but he did offer the complete elimination of all strategic weapons over the next ten years.[14] His condition was that the U.S. confine SDI research to "the laboratory," effectively killing it. He feared the U.S. would develop a working missile shield and then strike Russia before the end of the ten years.[15]

The crux of the matter was trust. Gorbachev did not believe the U.S. would share technology that would make nuclear arms irrelevant. Ultimately, negotiation between two superpowers had to be as Gorbachev stated: "We must both be winners." To achieve his goal, Reagan knew he had to be tough. He could not concede his principles (SDI), but he could not humiliate the Soviet Union. Gorbachev had to be able to come out of negotiations looking good.

Empowering leaders are consummate negotiators, not out of ego or trying to get their way—the need to win at all costs. Rather, they have a high ideal in mind. They focus on the ultimate good of the entire enterprise, industry, or organization. They think, act, and communicate strategically.

When empowering leaders have a big idea, a paradigm-shifting idea, they neither back down nor try to force the other person to their way of thinking. Instead, they find points of agreement, ideals on which they can both easily agree. From a position of agreement they can negotiate to their ultimate end.

———

On December 8, 1987 in Washington, D.C., Reagan and Gorbachev signed the INF Treaty. "It was a simple proposal one might say," said Reagan at the ceremony, "disarmingly simple. Unlike treaties in the past, it didn't simply codify the status quo or a new arms buildup; it didn't simply talk of controlling an arms race. For the first time in history, the language of 'arms control' was replaced by 'arms reduction'—in this case, the complete elimination of an entire class of U.S. and Soviet nuclear missiles." He then quoted the Russian maxim, "*Doveryai, no proveryai*—trust, but verify."

"You repeat that at every meeting," Gorbachev interrupted, chuckling.[16]

Reagan often used this well-known proverb of his "opponent." What better way to start with "yes, yes" than to appeal to a common maxim? Identifying a principle held in common is a first step to finding common ground.

George Shultz wrote that the INF treaty "was a watershed agreement, not only because of its terms but also because it showed that large-scale reductions in nuclear weapons were possible: the United States and the Soviets *could* work out a complex problem of great importance."[17] Reagan put into practice his belief that negotiations work best when the parties involved begin with "yes, yes." He dared to look for common ground with America's adversary, hoping to reach his own goal by appealing to common needs, fears, and dreams.

———

A president does not carry 49 states at reelection, winning the largest electoral vote in history, with narrow appeal. Reagan was a "Big Tent" person. He knew that to be successful, a political party needs to have a broad base of support. "While some in politics make lists of enemies," said Mike Deaver, "Reagan was forever bringing his foes 'under the tent.'"[18]

Reagan did not just start reaching out to people who normally voted Democratic in 1980 or 1984. Back in 1977 Reagan said to the Conservative Political Action Conference: "I want the record to show that I do not view the new revitalized Republican Party as one based on a principle of exclusion. After all, you do not get to be a majority party by searching for groups you won't associate or work with. If we truly believe in our principles, we should sit down and talk."[19]

In the 1980s the political landscape shifted as Reagan was supported by a significant number of traditionally Democratic voters. Known as the "Reagan Democrats," these voters realigned the electorate from leaning New Deal Democratic to Reagan Republican. These largely working-class voters were "disenchanted with rising marginal tax rates, high inflation, unemployment, and soaring interest rates."[20] Many were socially conservative Democrats in the South and the Midwest, disenchanted with the Democratic party's swing to the left in the 1960s and '70s.

Traditionally Democratic voters, as Reagan himself was for over half his life, were used to thinking of the Republican party as the party of big business and the Democratic party as that of laborers, immigrants, and the "common man." Reagan's own background as a struggling young man who admired FDR gave him a gut understanding of traditional working-class Democrats. He understood their values, needs, and concerns.

As a Republican candidate Reagan took care to show why he believed their social and economic interests were now best served by the Republican party. That the South and the Midwest are solidly Republican today testifies to Reagan's success in reaching out to Democratic and independent voters whose values he shared. As former ambassador to the United Nations (and life-long Democrat), Jeane Kirkpatrick said, "He understood well the phenomenon of the Reagan Democrat, because he was the first one!"[21]

Most senior management have worked with, if not started out as, minimum-wage laborers, often working summers in the field of their choice. It can be easy to forget what that experience was like, putting it behind you as you move on in your career. If you lose touch with that experience, you make a big mistake.

These members of your team will feel separated from the decision-making process. This hampers your ability to relate to them and their ability to relate to you. When you lose your mutual understanding and sense of connection, you have a tough time getting the "yes, yes" agreements that are essential in winning their cooperation and securing their engagement as you initiate change.

———

As an empowering leader, you can achieve more than you think. When you encounter objections or resistance, ask yourself, "Can the point be conceded without risking my main purpose?" When bringing others around to your way of thinking, make as many minor concessions as possible. If you can, modify your proposals to satisfy them. Advance your ideas in a modest way that invites agreement, not in a pushy manner that provokes opposition. Try to listen silently but politely when others attempt to force ideas upon you that you do not agree with.

If you face strong resistance to your main point, imitate Ronald Reagan: You might be wise to delay the issue. This gives the other party a chance to reconsider and provides you with an opportunity to reorganize your campaign. Have the patience to wait for your ultimate success while building trust and common ground. As Gorbachev said, "Reagan pushed me one step more and then one step more till we got to the precipice, and then he wanted one step more."[22]

Leadership Principle 15

"Whatever else history may say about me when I'm gone, I hope it will record that I appealed to your best hopes, not your worst fears; to your confidence rather than your doubts. My dream is that you will travel the road ahead with liberty's lamp guiding your steps and opportunity's arm steadying your way."

Ronald Reagan[1]

Appeal to Their Noble Motives

"People who talk about an age of limits," Reagan once said, "are really talking about their own limitations, not America's."[2] In his first inaugural address, January 20, 1981, Reagan said: "The crisis we are facing today...[requires] our willingness to believe in ourselves and to believe in our capacity to perform great deeds....And after all, why shouldn't we believe that? We are Americans."

Reagan always reminded us that our country's greatness comes from within ourselves. He felt his most important role as a leader was appealing to that greatness, and his mission was to draw that greatness out of us. He constantly reminded us of who we are, what we stand for, and why America's freedom works.

In his farewell address, January 11, 1989, he revisited many of the positive things that had happened in the previous eight years: the longest peacetime expansion in history to date, real family income up, more exports, advances in technology, the INF Treaty, and more.

Then Reagan said: "The lesson of all this was, of course, that because we're a great nation, our challenges seem complex. It will always be this way. But as long as we remember our first principles and believe in ourselves, the future will always be ours. And something else we learned: Once you begin a great movement, there's no telling where it will end. We meant to change a nation, and instead, we changed a world."[3]

Empowering leaders realize that the greatness of an organization is not "created" by management. Rather, it springs from the talent, skill, effort, and innovation of all members of the organization, united in common pursuit of the goal—achievement of your company's mission and fulfillment of your vision.

Empowering leaders help their team understand that what they are doing is not just changing a department, a company, or the lives of their associates. They are setting an example for others to follow. As empowering leaders, we become the benchmark against which future leaders will be measured and against which our team members will measure themselves.

Empowering leaders understand that they multiply their own strengths through others. They are not afraid of emerging leadership; they cultivate it. They help others grow, recognizing that others' growth is a reflection of their own leadership ability. It has been said that leadership is the scarcest resource on the planet. Yet, leadership can be exercised by everyone who has the courage of their convictions, the confidence to take the risks inherent in leadership, and the ability to influence others.

———

Reagan's 1980 campaign slogan was a good example of appealing to noble motives: "Let's Make America Great Again." Journalist Elizabeth Drew observed that "over the years, the Reagan campaigns have done better than any other at appropriating the patriotic symbols."[4]

This was not an accident. Reagan believed in bringing out the best in people by praising what is already good in them. He knew that praise can effect positive change. Reminding people of their greatness makes them want to do their best.

Empowering leaders like Ronald Reagan confront difficult situations and challenges by appealing to the high ideals of their team. The challenges of increasing competition facing all organizations lead to the necessity of ensuring maximum effort, team work, improved performance, and safety in a customer-focused way. Appealing to the noble nature, the high ideals, of others can help meet these challenges. People have a high regard for themselves and relish the satisfaction that comes from achieving stretch goals and breakthrough performance.

———

"The source of Reagan's vision," wrote Dinesh D'Souza, "was his possession of what Edmund Burke termed moral imagination. He saw the world through the clear lens of right and wrong. This kind of knowledge came not from books but from within himself....He was an apostle not so much of blind optimism as of hope."[5]

Reagan appealed to what he believed was good and right in the hope of inspiring people to bring it about in reality. This is your job as an empowering leader: appealing to the best, the most noble, in your associates, calling them to higher ground, the place where we all take pride in being.

To lead with greatest effect, appeal to the noble motives. Empowering leadership means bringing out the best so that results exceed high expectations. Authority can be granted through position or title, but leadership that others enthusiastically follow is always voluntary.

Appeal to the noble motives of your team by offering encouragement such as: "I can always trust you," "The team is counting on you," "You never let us down," "I appreciate your honesty and integrity." Let your ideals and values guide you in appreciating the ideals and values expressed by others.

———

In 1985 conservative thinkers Robert Novak and George Will heard Reagan speak about his hope of reaching the Soviet leader on a personal level and advancing U.S.-Soviet relations without compromising America's long-term security. Novak said that at the time, he and Will thought "it was foolish bordering on suicidal to think that the Soviet leaders would respond to personal initiatives. We thought...[t]he particular leader of the Soviet Union didn't matter, because it was the system that dictated policy. It was a bit of a shock, and an unpleasant one, to see that Reagan didn't share our view at all....It really makes you wonder, doesn't it? What did he know that we didn't?"[6]

Reagan had the vision and creativity to launch a new approach to U.S.-Soviet relations. He appealed to the humanity of Mikhail Gorbachev and challenged him to break away from the status quo. It was a daring departure from past presidents' approaches. Reagan dared to dream farther.

The "Reagan Doctrine" involved actively encouraging the reversal of Soviet gains, challenging the Brezhnev maxim of "once Communist, always Communist."[7] This approach, wrote Lady Margaret Thatcher, "demonstrated just how potent a weapon in international politics human rights could be. His view was that we should fight the battle of ideas for freedom against Communism throughout the world and refuse to accept the permanent exclusion of the captive nations from the benefits of freedom."[8]

Reagan dared to hope that the Soviet Union itself might one day be free. He hoped there was a human being like himself in the new general secretary and set out to find him. At Geneva, Reykjavík, and Washington, he treated Gorbachev like a man of reason, hope, and good-will. He adopted the Russian motto, "Trust, but verify," which powerfully expressed his way of dealing with the Soviet leader: Give people respect to induce them to be at their best, but be tough so that they also will respect you.

Reagan said that he was asked if America's "new closeness with the Soviet Union" "isn't a gamble." "[M]y answer is no," he replied, "because we're basing our actions not on words but deeds. The détente of the 1970s was based not on actions but promises....

"We must keep up our guard, but we must also continue to work together to lessen and eliminate tension and mistrust. My view is that President Gorbachev is different from previous Soviet leaders. I think he knows some of the things wrong with his society and is trying to fix them. We wish him well."[9]

Reagan won the respect of Gorbachev, and for the first time in three generations an American president and a Russian leader ultimately became personal friends. You, as an empowering leader, must break through the barrier of long-held beliefs about how things must be done: beliefs about labor and management, customers and suppliers, system limitations and processes requirements. Most importantly, you must come to believe in the greatness of your team. You must see the greatness so clearly that they begin to see it for themselves. This is empowering leadership at its best.

"We've done our part," said Reagan as he left the presidency. "And as I walk off into the city streets, a final word to the men and women of the Reagan revolution, the men and women across America who for eight years did the work that brought America back. My friends: We did it. We weren't just marking time. We made a difference. We made the city stronger, we made the city freer, and we left her in good hands. All in all, not bad, not bad at all."[10]

Empowering leaders bring joy, enthusiasm, and optimism into the world of those they touch everyday. As you lift others with your joy, you lift yourself. Take the initiative in tapping the noble motives of your team to bring the best out of them and improve performance on every level.

At the end of each endeavor, every project, any milestone, you too can say to your team, your department, your organization, "My friends: We did it." As an empowering leader, you can take pride in your team's achievements and celebrate their successes. When you appeal to the best in others, you reap the rewards of advancing toward the accomplishment of your goals, the realization of your vision, and the achievement of your mission.

Notes

Introduction

[1] Ronald Reagan Presidential Library Foundation, *Mourning in America* (Simi Valley, California, 2004), video tribute.

[2] At the Republican National Convention, New York City.

[3] Peter Robinson, "'Morning Again in America,'" *The Wall Street Journal* (7 June 2004).

[4] Ronald Reagan Presidential Library Foundation.

[5] Ibid.

[6] Ibid.

[7] Address to the Fourth Annual Conservative Political Action Conference (February 6, 1977); in Ronald Reagan, *The Greatest Speeches of Ronald Reagan*, with an introduction by Michael Reagan, (West Palm Beach, Florida: NewsMax.com, 2002), 63.

[8] Edwin Meese III, *With Reagan: The Inside Story* (Washington, D.C.: Regnery Gateway, 1992), 331.

[9] Ronald Reagan Presidential Library Foundation.

Principle One: Lead from High Ideals

[1] Peggy Noonan, *When Character Was King: A Story of Ronald Reagan* (New York: Viking, 2001), 317.

[2] Peter Schweizer, *Reagan's War: The Epic Story of His Forty-Year Struggle and Final Triumph over Communism* (New York: Doubleday, 2002), 270.

[3] Peter Robinson, "'Morning Again in America,'" *The Wall Street Journal* (7 June 2004).

[4] Michael Reagan, introduction to Ronald Reagan, *The Greatest Speeches of Ronald Reagan*, with an introduction by Michael Reagan (West Palm Beach, Florida: NewsMax.com, 2002), ix-x.

[5] Peter Hannaford, ed., *Recollections of Reagan: A Portrait of Ronald Reagan* (New York: William Morrow and Company, 1997), 73.

[6] Ronald Reagan, *Speaking My Mind* (Norwalk, Connecticut: The Easton Press, 1989), 85.

[7] Ann Reilly Dowd, "What Managers Can Learn from Manager Reagan," reprinted in Paul Boyer, ed., *Reagan as President: Contemporary Views of the Man, His Politics, and His Policies* (Chicago: Dee, 1990), 6; quoted in James M. Strock, *Reagan on Leadership: Executive Lessons from the Great Communicator* (Rocklin, California: Prima Publishing, 1998), 138.

[8] Ronald Reagan, *An American Life* (New York: Simon and Schuster, 1990), 247.

[9] Strock, 125.

[10] Robert V. Friedenberg, *Notable Speeches in Contemporary Presidential Campaigns* (Westport, Connecticut: Praeger Publishers, 2002), 162.

[11] Ronald Reagan Presidential Foundation, *Ronald Reagan: An American Hero*, with reflections by Nancy Reagan (New York: Dorling Kindersley Publishing, 2001), 253.

[12] Hannaford, 44.

[13] Ibid., 71.

[14] Lou Cannon, *Reagan* (New York: G. P. Putnam's Sons, 1982), 13; and Friedenberg, 143.

[15] "A Time for Choosing," (October 27, 1964); in Reagan, *The Greatest Speeches of Ronald Reagan*, 1, 4.

[16] Edwin Meese III, *With Reagan: The Inside Story* (Washington, D.C.: Regnery Gateway, 1992), 19-20.

[17] Hannaford, 186.

[18] Laurence Barrett, *Gambling with History* (New York: Doubleday, 1983); in Meese, 18.

[19] Meese, 331.

[20] Peter Robinson, *How Ronald Reagan Changed My Life* (New York: ReganBooks, 2003), 112-113.

[21] Farewell address to the nation (January 11, 1989); in Reagan, 247.

[22] Dinesh D'Souza, *Ronald Reagan: How an Ordinary Man Became an Extraordinary Leader* (New York: The Free Press, 1997), 4.

Principle Two: Become Genuinely Interested

[1] Kiron K. Skinner, Annelise Anderson, and Martin Anderson, ed., *Reagan: A Life in Letters*, with a foreword by George P. Shultz (New York: Free Press, 2003), 657.

[2] Michael K. Deaver, *A Different Drummer: My Thirty Years with Ronald Reagan*, with a foreword by Nancy Reagan (New York: HarperCollins Publishers, 2001), 177.

[3] Ronald Reagan, *An American Life* (New York: Simon and Schuster, 1990), 52.

[4] Deaver, 182.

[5] Reagan, 89-90.

[6] Ibid., 90.

[7] Ibid.

[8] Lou Cannon, *Reagan* (New York: G. P. Putnam's Sons, 1982), 92; and Reagan, 131.

[9] Peter Robinson, *How Ronald Reagan Changed My Life* (New York: ReganBooks, 2003), 119.

[10] Peter Hannaford, ed., *Recollections of Reagan: A Portrait of Ronald Reagan* (New York: William Morrow and Company, 1997), 108-109.

[11] Robinson, 120.

[12] Helen Thomas, *Front Row at the White House: My Life and Times* (New York: Scribner, 1999), 335.

[13] Dinesh D'Souza, *Ronald Reagan: How an Ordinary Man Became an Extraordinary Leader* (New York: The Free Press, 1997), 216.

[14] Ralph E. Weber and Ralph A. Weber, ed., *Dear Americans: Letters from the Desk of President Ronald Reagan* (New York: Doubleday, 2003), 4.

[15] D'Souza, 217.

[16] Hannaford, 127.

[17] Ibid., 153.

[18] Ibid., 154.

[19] Ibid., 137.

[20] D'Souza, 215.

[21] Edwin Meese III, *With Reagan: The Inside Story* (Washington, D.C.: Regnery Gateway, 1992), 330.

[22] Ibid., xviii.

[23] Robinson, 5-6.

[24] Deaver, 54.

[25] Ibid., 122.

Principle Three: Don't Criticize, Condemn, or Complain

[1] 1984; Bill Adler and Bill Adler, Jr., ed., *The Reagan Wit: The Humor of the American President* (New York: William Morrow and Company, 1998), 148.

[2] Peter Schweizer, *Reagan's War: The Epic Story of His Forty-Year Struggle and Final Triumph over Communism* (New York: Doubleday, 2002), 50.

[3] Dinesh D'Souza, *Ronald Reagan: How an Ordinary Man Became an Extraordinary Leader* (New York: The Free Press, 1997), 264.

[4] Peggy Noonan, *What I Saw at the Revolution: A Political Life in the Reagan Era* (New York: Random House, 1990), 57.

[5] Larry Speakes, *Speaking Out: The Reagan Presidency from Inside the White House*, with Robert Pack (New York: Scribner, 1988), 104; quoted in James M. Strock, *Reagan on Leadership: Executive Lessons from the Great Communicator* (Rocklin, California: Prima Publishing, 1998), 221-222.

[6] Adler and Adler, 93.

[7] D'Souza, 103; and Lou Cannon, *President Reagan: The Role of a Lifetime* (New York: Simon and Schuster, 1991), 130.

[8] Adler and Adler, 15.

[9] 1969; ibid., 39.

[10] Helen Thomas, *Thanks for the Memories, Mr. President: Wit and Wisdom from the Front Row at the White House* (New York: Scribner, 2002), 131.

[11] Adler and Adler, 138.

[12] Peter Hannaford, ed., *Recollections of Reagan: A Portrait of Ronald Reagan* (New York: William Morrow and Company, 1997), 167.

[13] Ibid., 58.

[14] Ibid., 33.

[15] Thomas, 130.

[16] 1967; Bill Adler, ed., *The Reagan Wit*, with Bill Adler, Jr. (Aurora, Illinois: Caroline House Publishers, 1981), 59.

[17] Helen Thomas, *Front Row at the White House: My Life and Times* (New York: Scribner, 1999), 344.

[18] Hannaford, 41.

[19] Meese, 17.

[20] Ibid., 25.

[21] Deaver, 163-164.

[22] Ralph E. Weber and Ralph A. Weber, ed., *Dear Americans: Letters from the Desk of President Ronald Reagan* (New York: Doubleday, 2003), 199.

[23] Noonan, 151.

[24] Nancy Reagan, *My Turn*, with William Novak (New York: Random House, 1989), 108.

[25] Ibid.

[26] Hannaford, 117.

Principle Four: Provide Acknowledgment

[1] Paul D. Erickson, *Reagan Speaks* (New York: New York University Press, 1985), 106-107.

[2] Helen Thomas, *Front Row at the White House: My Life and Times* (New York: Scribner, 1999), 344.

[3] Peggy Noonan, *When Character Was King: A Story of Ronald Reagan* (New York: Viking, 2001), 49.

[4] Peter Schweizer, *Reagan's War: The Epic Story of His Forty-Year Struggle and Final Triumph over Communism* (New York: Doubleday, 2002), 5.

[5] Noonan, 50.

[6] Dinesh D'Souza, *Ronald Reagan: How an Ordinary Man Became an Extraordinary Leader* (New York: The Free Press, 1997), 215.

[7] Ibid., 215-216.

[8] Margaret Thatcher, *The Downing Street Years* (New York: HarperCollins Publishers, 1993), 435.

[9] Noonan, 234-235.

[10] Edwin Meese III, *With Reagan: The Inside Story* (Washington, D.C.: Regnery Gateway, 1992), xvii.

[11] Ronald Reagan, *An American Life* (New York: Simon and Schuster, 1990), 638.

[12] Address at the dedication of the Westminster College Cold War Memorial, Fulton, Missouri (November 19, 1990); in Ronald Reagan, *The Greatest Speeches of Ronald Reagan*, with an introduction by Michael Reagan (West Palm Beach, Florida: NewsMax.com, 2002), 262.

[13] Ibid.

[14] Michael K. Deaver, *A Different Drummer: My Thirty Years with Ronald Reagan*, with a foreward by Nancy Reagan (New York: HarperCollins Publishers, 2001), 86-87.

[15] Ibid., 87-88.

[16] Peter Hannaford, ed., *Recollections of Reagan: A Portrait of Ronald Reagan* (New York: William Morrow and Company, 1997), 142.

[17] Ibid., 143.

[18] Caspar W. Weinberger, *In the Arena: A Memoir of the 20th Century*, with Gretchen Roberts (Washington, D.C.: Regnery Publishing, 2001), 277-278.

[19] June 6, 1984; in Reagan, *The Greatest Speeches of Ronald Reagan*, 205-206.

[20] Hannaford, 29.

[21] Peggy Noonan, *What I Saw at the Revolution: A Political Life in the Reagan Era* (New York: Random House, 1990), 253-259.

[22] Nancy Reagan, *My Turn*, with William Novak (New York: Random House, 1989), 10.

[23] Hannaford, 80.

[24] Kiron K. Skinner, Annelise Anderson, and Martin Anderson, ed., *Stories in His Own Hand: The Everyday Wisdom of Ronald Reagan*, with a foreword by George P. Shultz (New York: The Free Press, 2001), 62-64.

[25] Peter Robinson, *How Ronald Reagan Changed My Life* (New York: ReganBooks, 2003), 258-259.

Principle Five: See Their Point of View

[1] Address at the Brandenburg Gate, West Berlin (June 12, 1987); in Ronald Reagan, *The Greatest Speeches of Ronald Reagan*, with an introduction by Michael Reagan (West Palm Beach, Florida: NewsMax.com, 2002), 236.

[2] Peter Robinson, *How Ronald Reagan Changed My Life* (New York: ReganBooks, 2003), 246-247.

[3] Ronald Reagan Presidential Foundation, *Ronald Reagan: An American Hero*, with reflections by Nancy Reagan (New York: Dorling Kindersley Publishing, 2001), 209.

[4] Ronald Reagan, *An American Life* (New York: Simon and Schuster, 1990), 42.

[5] Michael K. Deaver, *A Different Drummer: My Thirty Years with Ronald Reagan*, with a foreword by Nancy Reagan (New York: HarperCollins Publishers, 2001), 4-5.

[6] Peter Hannaford, ed., *Recollections of Reagan: A Portrait of Ronald Reagan* (New York: William Morrow and Company, 1997), 146.

[7] Dinesh D'Souza, *Ronald Reagan: How an Ordinary Man Became an Extraordinary Leader* (New York: The Free Press, 1997), 216.

[8] Kiron K. Skinner, Annelise Anderson, and Martin Anderson, ed., *Reagan: A Life in Letters*, with a foreword by George P. Shultz (New York: Free Press, 2003), xiii.

[9] Ibid., xv.

[10] Hannaford, 31.

[11] Ralph E. Weber and Ralph A. Weber, ed., *Dear Americans: Letters from the Desk of President Ronald Reagan* (New York: Doubleday, 2003), 356-357.

[12] Skinner, Anderson, and Anderson, xv.

[13] Hannaford, 176.

[14] Reagan, 162.

[15] George Bush, *All the Best, George Bush* (New York: Scribner, 1999), 327.

[16] Deaver, 109-111.

[17] Margaret Thatcher, *The Downing Street Years* (New York: HarperCollins Publishers, 1993), 330-335.

[18] Deaver, 46-47.

[19] Reagan, 376-377.

[20] Deaver, 106-107.

[21] Michael K. Deaver, *Behind the Scenes*, with Mickey Herskowitz (New York: William Morrow and Company, 1987), 180-190.

[22] Lyn Nofziger, *Nofziger* (Washington, D.C.: Regnery Gateway, 1992), 295.

[23] Ibid., 293.

Principle Six: Be an Active Listener

[1] Ronald Reagan, *An American Life* (New York: Simon and Schuster, 1990), 129.

[2] Peggy Noonan, *When Character Was King: A Story of Ronald Reagan* (New York: Viking, 2001), 26-27.

[3] Lou Cannon, *President Reagan: The Role of a Lifetime* (New York: Simon and Schuster, 1991), 89; General Electric website, *General Electric*, <http://www.ge.com/en/> and <http://www.ge.com/en/company/companyinfo/at_a_glance/r eagan_speech.htm> (12 September 2004); Robert V. Friedenberg, *Notable Speeches in Contemporary Presidential Campaigns* (Westport, Connecticut: Praeger Publishers, 2002), 147; and Ronald Reagan Presidential Foundation,

Ronald Reagan: An American Hero, with reflections by Nancy Reagan (New York: Dorling Kindersley Publishing, 2001), 114-115.

[4] Michael K. Deaver, *A Different Drummer: My Thirty Years with Ronald Reagan*, with a foreward by Nancy Reagan (New York: HarperCollins Publishers, 2001), 19.

[5] Elizabeth Drew, *Portrait of an Election* (New York: Simon and Schuster, 1981), 113; cited in Friedenberg, 152.

[6] Friedenberg, 150; and Reagan, 151-152.

[7] Deaver, 53-54.

[8] Ibid., 74; and Reagan, 248.

[9] Reagan, 247.

[10] Deaver, 52-53.

[11] Ronald Reagan Presidential Foundation, 188.

[12] Peter Hannaford, ed., *Recollections of Reagan: A Portrait of Ronald Reagan* (New York: William Morrow and Company, 1997), 86.

[13] Deaver, 35-36.

[14] Tip O'Neill, *Man of the House*, with William Novak (New York: Random House, 1987), 341-342.

[15] Hannaford, 48.

[16] Lou Cannon, *Reagan* (New York: G. P. Putnam's Sons, 1982), 154; emphasis added.

[17] Deaver, 101-103; and Michael K. Deaver, *Behind the Scenes*, with Mickey Herskowitz (New York: William Morrow and Company, 1987), 165-166.

[18] Reagan, 184.

Principle Seven: Play Yourself Down

[1] Actor Robert Cummings; quoted in Ronald Reagan Presidential Foundation, *Ronald Reagan: An American Hero*, with reflections by Nancy Reagan (New York: Dorling Kindersley Publishing, 2001), 84.

[2] Michael K. Deaver, *A Different Drummer: My Thirty Years with Ronald Reagan*, with a foreward by Nancy Reagan (New York: HarperCollins Publishers, 2001), 76-77.

[3] Nancy Reagan, *My Turn*, with William Novak (New York: Random House, 1989), 112.

[4] Peter J. Wallison, *Ronald Reagan: The Power of Conviction and the Success of His Presidency* (Boulder, Colorado: Westview Press, 2003), x.

[5] Deaver, 62.

[6] Ibid., 159.

[7] David Gergen, *Eyewitness to Power: The Essence of Leadership* (New York: Simon and Schuster, 2000), 152-153.

[8] Deaver, 157.

[9] Ibid.; and Ronald Reagan Presidential Foundation, 127.

[10] Caspar W. Weinberger in Peter Hannaford, ed., *Recollections of Reagan: A Portrait of Ronald Reagan* (New York: William Morrow and Company, 1997), 185.

[11] Wilson D. Miscamble, C.S.C., *Go Forth and Do Good: Memorable Notre Dame Commencement Addresses* (Notre Dame, Indiana: University of Notre Dame Press, 2003), 207.

[12] Reagan, 95.

[13] Marcus Winters, "A Conversation with Edwin Meese," *Libertas: The Voice of Freedom on Campus* (Young

233

America's Foundation newsletter, Commemorative Reagan Edition 2004): 5.

[14] Peggy Noonan, *When Character Was King: A Story of Ronald Reagan* (New York: Viking, 2001), 133.

[15] Ibid.

[16] Hannaford, 27.

[17] Tip O'Neill, *Man of the House*, with William Novak (New York: Random House, 1987), 335.

[18] Ibid., 331-332.

[19] Ibid., 333.

[20] Edwin Meese III, *With Reagan: The Inside Story* (Washington, D.C.: Regnery Gateway, 1992), 25.

[21] 1980; Bill Adler and Bill Adler, Jr., ed., *The Reagan Wit: The Humor of the American President* (New York: William Morrow and Company, 1998), 85.

[22] Deaver, 70.

[23] Helen Thomas, *Thanks for the Memories, Mr. President* (New York: Scribner, 2002), 132.

[24] At the White House Correspondents Association Dinner, Washington, D.C. (April 1987); Adler and Adler, 151.

[25] Thomas, 127.

[26] Deaver, 141; and Dinesh D'Souza, *Ronald Reagan: How an Ordinary Man Became an Extraordinary Leader* (New York: The Free Press, 1997), 206.

[27] Thomas, 135.

[28] Deaver, 188.

[29] Thomas, 142.

[30] Told during an address before the World Affairs Council (1988); Noonan, 236; also Adler and Adler, 162-163.

Principle Eight: Validate Their Ideas

[1] David Gergen, *Eyewitness to Power: The Essence of Leadership* (New York: Simon and Schuster, 2000), 168.

[2] Robert V. Friedenberg, *Notable Speeches in Contemporary Presidential Campaigns* (Westport, Connecticut: Praeger Publishers, 2002), 156.

[3] Gergen, 169.

[4] Nancy Reagan, *My Turn*, with William Novak (New York: Random House, 1989), 353.

[5] Peter Hannaford, ed., *Recollections of Reagan: A Portrait of Ronald Reagan* (New York: William Morrow and Company, 1997), 165.

[6] Tip O'Neill, *Man of the House*, with William Novak (New York: Random House, 1987), 342-343.

[7] Hannaford, 86.

[8] Donald T. Regan, *For the Record: From Wall Street to Washington* (New York: Harcourt Brace Jovanovich, Publishers, 1988), 143-144, 157.

[9] Peter J. Wallison, *Ronald Reagan: The Power of Conviction and the Success of His Presidency* (Boulder, Colorado: Westview Press, 2003), 16-17.

[10] Ronald Reagan, *An American Life* (New York: Simon and Schuster, 1990), 161.

[11] Margaret Thatcher, *The Downing Street Years* (New York: HarperCollins Publishers, 1993), 157.

[12] February 6, 1977; in Ronald Reagan, *The Greatest Speeches of Ronald Reagan*, with an introduction by Michael Reagan (West Palm Beach, Florida: NewsMax.com, 2001), 66-67.

[13] Michael K. Deaver, *A Different Drummer: My Thirty Years with Ronald Reagan*, with a foreward by Nancy Reagan (New York: HarperCollins Publishers, 2001), 33.

[14] Gergen, 161.

[15] Edwin Meese III, *With Reagan: The Inside Story* (Washington, D.C.: Regnery Gateway, 1992), 127.

[16] Gergen, 163.

[17] Dinesh D'Souza, *Ronald Reagan: How an Ordinary Man Became an Extraordinary Leader* (New York: The Free Press, 1997), 21.

Principle Nine: Dramatize Your Ideas

[1] Ronald Reagan, *Speaking My Mind: Selected Speeches* (Norwalk, Connecticut: The Easton Press, 1989), 30.

[2] Ronald Reagan, *An American Life* (New York: Simon and Schuster, 1990), 182-183.

[3] Reagan, *Speaking My Mind: Selected Speeches*, 76.

[4] Peggy Noonan, *What I Saw at the Revolution: A Political Life in the Reagan Era* (New York: Random House, 1990), 125.

[5] Ronald Reagan Presidential Foundation, *Ronald Reagan: An American Hero*, with reflections by Nancy Reagan (New York: Dorling Kindersley Publishing, 2001), 9.

[6] Reagan, *An American Life*, 59.

[7] Ibid., 63-65.

[8] Ibid., 65-66.

[9] Michael K. Deaver, *A Different Drummer: My Thirty Years with Ronald Reagan*, with a foreward by Nancy Reagan (New York: HarperCollins Publishers, 2001), 83.

[10] Bill Adler and Bill Adler, Jr., ed., *The Reagan Wit: The Humor of the American President* (New York: William Morrow and Company, 1998), 53.

[11] Stephen Vaughn, *Ronald Reagan in Hollywood* (New York: Cambridge University Press, 1964), 23-24.

[12] Ibid., 221.

[13] Ibid., 222; emphasis added.

[14] Lou Cannon, *President Reagan: The Role of a Lifetime* (New York: Simon and Schuster, 1991), 513.

[15] First inaugural address (January 20, 1981); in Reagan, *Speaking My Mind: Selected Speeches*, 65.

[16] Paul D. Erickson, *Reagan Speaks* (New York: New York University Press, 1985), 107-108.

[17] Noonan, 146.

[18] Peter Hannaford, ed., *Recollections of Reagan: A Portrait of Ronald Reagan* (New York: William Morrow and Company, 1997), 63-64.

[19] Ken Adelman, "The Real Reagan," *The Wall Street Journal* (5 October 1999).

[20] Ibid.

[21] Hannaford, 47.

[22] Wilson D. Miscamble, C.S.C., *Go Forth and Do Good: Memorable Notre Dame Commencement Addresses* (Notre Dame, Indiana: University of Notre Dame Press, 2003), 209.

[23] Farewell address to the nation (January 11, 1989); in Reagan, 410-411.

[24] Reagan, *An American Life*, 246.

Principle Ten: Stimulate Competition

[1] June 12, 1987.

[2] Address to the Annual Convention of the National Association of Evangelicals, Orlando, Florida (March 8, 1983); in Ronald Reagan, *The Greatest Speeches of Ronald Reagan*, with an introduction by Michael Reagan (West Palm Beach, Florida: NewsMax.com, 2001), 153.

[3] Dinesh D'Souza, *Ronald Reagan: How an Ordinary Man Became an Extraordinary Leader* (New York: The Free Press, 1997), 29.

[4] Ibid., 30.

[5] Ibid., 30-31.

[6] David Gergen, *Eyewitness to Power: The Essence of Leadership* (New York: Simon and Schuster, 2000), 183.

[7] June 12, 1987; in Reagan, 234-235, 237.

[8] Houston, Texas (August 17, 1992); ibid., 276.

Principle Eleven: When You Blow It, Show It

[1] October 15, 1974; Bill Adler and Bill Adler, Jr., ed., *The Reagan Wit: The Humor of the American President* (New York: William Morrow and Company, 1998), 65.

[2] Dinesh D'Souza, *Ronald Reagan: How an Ordinary Man Became an Extraordinary Leader* (New York: The Free Press, 1997), 216.

[3] Michael K. Deaver, *A Different Drummer: My Thirty Years with Ronald Reagan*, with a foreward by Nancy Reagan (New York: HarperCollins Publishers, 2001), 154.

[4] Ronald Reagan, *An American Life* (New York: Simon and Schuster, 1990), 640.

[5] Peter Hannaford, ed., *Recollections of Reagan: A Portrait of Ronald Reagan* (New York: William Morrow and Company, 1997), 127.

[6] D'Souza, 10.

[7] Hannaford, xii.

[8] Deaver, 64-65.

[9] Ibid., 65-67.

[10] Ibid., 186-187.

[11] January 17, 1968; Adler and Adler, 56.

[12] Bill Adler, ed., with Bill Adler, Jr., *The Reagan Wit* (Aurora, Illinois: Caroline House Publishers, 1981), 73.

[13] Address to the nation (March 4, 1987); in Ronald Reagan, *The Greatest Speeches of Ronald Reagan*, with an introduction by Michael Reagan (West Palm Beach, Florida: NewsMax.com, 2001), 224-229.

[14] George P. Shultz, *Turmoil and Triumph: My Years As Secretary of State* (New York: Charles Scribner's Sons, 1993), 908.

[15] Ralph E. Weber and Ralph A. Weber, ed., *Dear Americans: Letters from the Desk of President Ronald Reagan* (New York: Doubleday, 2003), 322.

[16] Peter J. Wallison, *Ronald Reagan: The Power of Conviction and the Success of His Presidency* (Boulder, Colorado: Westview Press, 2003), 281-282.

[17] Ronald Reagan Presidential Foundation, *Ronald Reagan: An American Hero*, with reflections by Nancy Reagan (New York: Dorling Kindersley Publishing, 2001), 245.

Principle Twelve: Avoid Dogmatic Declarations

[1] Ronald Reagan, *An American Life* (New York: Simon and Schuster, 1990), 637.

[2] Peter Hannaford, ed., *Recollections of Reagan: A Portrait of Ronald Reagan* (New York: William Morrow and Company, 1997), 69.

[3] Charlton Heston, *In the Arena: An Autobiography* (New York: Simon and Schuster, 1995), 237.

[4] Ibid.

[5] Ibid., 238.

[6] Address to the Fourth Annual Conservative Political Action Conference (February 6, 1977); in Ronald Reagan, *The Greatest Speeches of Ronald Reagan*, with an introduction by Michael Reagan (West Palm Beach, Florida: NewsMax.com, 2001), 52-54

[7] January 20, 1981; ibid., 93.

[8] Edwin Meese III, *With Reagan: The Inside Story* (Washington, D.C.: Regnery Gateway, 1992), 20.

[9] Ibid., 21.

[10] Ibid., 20-21.

[11] George P. Shultz, *Turmoil and Triumph: My Years As Secretary of State* (New York: Charles Scribner's Sons, 1993), 775.

[12] Lyn Nofziger, *Nofziger* (Washington, D.C.: Regnery Gateway, 1992), 46.

[13] Dinesh D'Souza, *Ronald Reagan: How an Ordinary Man Became an Extraordinary Leader* (New York: The Free Press, 1997), 30.

[14] James M. Strock, *Reagan on Leadership: Executive Lessons from the Great Communicator* (Rocklin, California: Prima Publishing, 1998), 70.

Principle Thirteen: Avoid Arguments

[1] Helen Thomas, *Thanks for the Memories, Mr. President* (New York: Scribner, 2002), 139.

[2] Commemorating the Bicentennial Year of Air and Space Flight (1983); in Ronald Reagan, *The Greatest Speeches of Ronald Reagan*, with an introduction by Michael Reagan (West Palm Beach, Florida: NewsMax.com, 2001), 150.

[3] Margaret Thatcher, *The Downing Street Years* (New York: HarperCollins Publishers, 1993), 158.

[4] Michael K. Deaver, *A Different Drummer: My Thirty Years with Ronald Reagan*, with a foreward by Nancy Reagan (New York: HarperCollins Publishers, 2001), 109.

[5] Ibid.

[6] Ibid.

[7] Ronald Reagan, *An American Life* (New York: Simon and Schuster, 1990), 639.

[8] Edwin Meese III, *With Reagan: The Inside Story* (Washington, D.C.: Regnery Gateway, 1992), 14.

[9] Ibid.

[10] Ronald Reagan Presidential Foundation, *Ronald Reagan: An American Hero*, with reflections by Nancy Reagan (New York: Dorling Kindersley Publishing, 2001), 24.

[11] Lou Cannon, *Reagan* (New York: G. P. Putnam's Sons, 1982), 118.

[12] Bill Adler and Bill Adler, Jr., ed., *The Reagan Wit: The Humor of the American President* (New York: William Morrow and Company, 1998), 139.

[13] Robert V. Friedenberg, *Notable Speeches in Contemporary Presidential Campaigns* (Westport, Connecticut: Praeger Publishers, 2002), 154-155.

[14] Thomas, 141.

[15] Peter J. Wallison, *Ronald Reagan: The Power of Conviction and the Success of His Presidency* (Boulder, Colorado: Westview Press, 2003), 11.

[16] George H. W. Bush, "'Strong, Strong Beliefs,'" *Newsweek*, 21 June 2004.

Principle Fourteen: Begin with Yes, Yes

[1] Dinesh D'Souza, *Ronald Reagan: How an Ordinary Man Became an Extraordinary Leader* (New York: The Free Press, 1997), 123.

[2] Tip O'Neill, *Man of the House*, with William Novak (New York: Random House, 1987), 373.

[3] D'Souza, 123.

[4] O'Neill, 374.

[5] June 12, 1987; in Ronald Reagan, *The Greatest Speeches of Ronald Reagan*, with an introduction by Michael Reagan (West Palm Beach, Florida: NewsMax.com, 2001), 236.

[6] Ronald Reagan, *An American Life* (New York: Simon and Schuster, 1990), 12.

[7] Ibid., 637.

[8] Ibid., 13.

[9] Ibid., 636.

[10] Ken Adelman, "The Real Reagan," *The Wall Street Journal* (5 October 1999).

[11] George P. Shultz, *Turmoil and Triumph: My Years As Secretary of State* (New York: Charles Scribner's Sons, 1993), 775.

[12] James M. Strock, *Reagan on Leadership: Executive Lessons from the Great Communicator* (Rocklin, California: Prima Publishing, 1998), 62.

[13] Shultz, 772, 771.

[14] Ibid., 761, 771.

[15] Ibid., 770.

[16] Ibid., 1009-1010.

[17] Ibid., 1130-1131.

[18] Michael K. Deaver, *A Different Drummer: My Thirty Years with Ronald Reagan*, with a foreward by Nancy Reagan (New York: HarperCollins Publishers, 2001), 4, 20.

[19] Address to the Fourth Annual Conservative Political Action Conference (February 6, 1977); in Reagan, *The Greatest Speeches of Ronald Reagan*, 65.

[20] Thomas Byrne Edsall, "The Reagan Legacy," in Sidney Blumenthal and Thomas Byrne Edsall, ed., *The Reagan Legacy* (New York: Pantheon Books, 1988), 9.

[21] Peter Hannaford, ed., *Recollections of Reagan: A Portrait of Ronald Reagan* (New York: William Morrow and Company, 1997), 79.

[22] Ronald Reagan Presidential Foundation, *Ronald Reagan: An American Hero*, with reflections by Nancy Reagan (New York: Dorling Kindersley Publishing, 2001), 210.

Principle Fifteen: Appeal to Their Noble Motives

[1] Address to the Republican National Convention, Houston, Texas (August 17, 1992); in Ronald Reagan, *The Greatest Speeches of Ronald Reagan*, with an introduction by Michael Reagan, (West Palm Beach, Florida: NewsMax.com, 2002), 276.

[2] Peter J. Wallison, *Ronald Reagan: The Power of Conviction and the Success of His Presidency* (Boulder, Colorado: Westview Press, 2003), 15.

[3] Farewell address to the nation (January 11, 1989); in Reagan, 247-248.

[4] Elizabeth Drew, *Portrait of an Election* (New York: Simon and Schuster, 1981), 113; quoted in Robert V. Friedenberg, *Notable Speeches in Contemporary Presidential Campaigns* (Westport, Connecticut: Praeger Publishers, 2002), 152.

[5] Dinesh D'Souza, *Ronald Reagan: How an Ordinary Man Became an Extraordinary Leader* (New York: The Free Press, 1997), 28.

[6] Ibid., 1-2.

[7] Ibid., 152.

[8] Margaret Thatcher, *The Path to Power* (New York: HarperCollins Publishers, 1995), 527-528.

[9] Farewell address to the nation (January 11, 1989); in Reagan, 250.

[10] Ibid., 253-254.

About The Author

Larry W. Dennis is the energetic founder of Turbo Leadership Systems™. The author of the successful books, *Repeat Business, How To Turbo Charge You, Empowering Leadership, InFormation, Making Moments Matter*, the children's book *The Great Baseball Cap*, and *Motorcycle Meditations*. Over the past 30+ years, Larry has been responsible for improving the performance and profits for hundreds of organizations whose leaders have developed skills in teamwork, customer service, and empowering leadership. Larry is also the inventor of the patented video training system, Psycho-Actualized Learning (PAL), a dedicated father who has been profiled in "Secrets of Raising Teenagers Successfully." He is listed in *Who's Who of the World* and serves on the boards of his church, the Providence Newberg Health Foundation, and Cascade Policy Institute. He is a member of the International Platform Association and the National Speaker's Association.

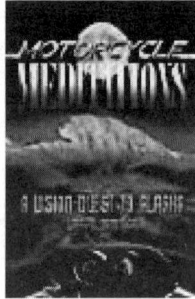

<u>Motorcycle Meditations - A Vision Quest to Alaska</u>

Share Larry W. Dennis, Sr.'s adventure of a lifetime. Ride along and experience his journey through Canada on the Al-Can and on through Alaska to Anchorage and Homer. You will experience the power of positive introspection, reflect and ponder your own life, rediscover the richness and gifts your life has given you. You will experience with great joy the promise of the present moments in your life. You will see with fresh eyes the promise of your future.

ISBN 0-9631766-6-8 $19.95

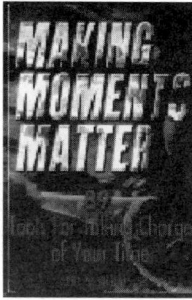

MAKING MOMENTS MATTER provides powerful time management tools to help you become more organized and productive in your professional and personal lives. 89 time management tools provide insight into how to make the most of every precious minute of every day.

Second Printing   ISBN 0-9631766-4-4 $16.95

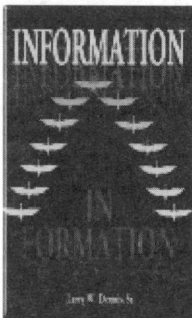

InFormation – How To Gain the 71% Advantage equips your team with the same advantage a flock of geese takes for granted. By following the tested guidelines outlined in this authentic resource book, your organization will fly farther, faster, and with no additional effort, keeping you out in front.

Second Printing   ISBN 0-9631766-3-3 $19.95

EMPOWERING LEADERSHIP helps you understand the Fifteen Fundamental Leadership Principles needed to tap your team's full potential. You see how to bring out the best in yourself and others. Whether you are a manager, supervisor, team leader or committee chair, you are shown how to exercise empowering leadership.

Fourth Printing   ISBN 0-9631766-1-7 $24.95

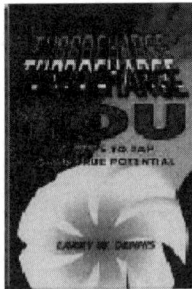

HOW TO TURBO CHARGE YOU - 6 STEPS TO TAP YOUR TRUE POTENTIAL guides you to an understanding of your unique talents and abilities. You see for the first time how to leverage your past successes. Written with real life examples, in an entertaining style, *How to Turbo Charge You* equips you with the 14 tools needed to thrive in a time of uncertainty and accelerated change.

Fourth Printing   ISBN 0-9631766-2-5 $14.95

REPEAT BUSINESS – 6 STEPS TO SUPERIOR CUSTOMER SERVICE teaches your new and long-term employees the skills that will help you create loyal customers. Written in straightforward, plain language and colorful anecdotes, *Repeat Business* helps you learn how to treat people so they keep coming back as satisfied customers.

Fifth Printing   ISBN 0-9631766-0-9 $9.95

THE GREAT BASEBALL CAP - This 32-page character building children's story is illustrated with warm 5-color pencil drawings. *The Great Baseball Cap* inspires 4 to 12-year old readers to take pride in their personal appearance, value relationships with their parents, siblings, and friends, and most important of all, value themselves. *The Great Baseball Cap* literally takes the young reader to the point of affirming **"I AM A WINNER!"**

ISBN 0-9631766-5-X $9.95

TURBO LEADERSHIP SYSTEMS PROCESSES

Cultural Benchmark Survey (CBS): Organizational strengths are analyzed for clarity and focus. Customer Opinion and Employee Opinion Surveys measure strengths and weaknesses of your organization. This provides direction for breakthroughs and continuous performance improvement.

Leadership Team Advance (LTA): Senior leadership team assesses its strengths and areas for needed improvement. The leadership team aligns its efforts with organizational objectives, and prepares to align all departments. Senior team members develop action plans with built-in follow-up and accountabilities to insure immediate results and sustained performance improvement.

Cultural Quality Awareness (CQA): The entire company experiences a "milestone day," establishing continuous improvement as a way of life. Suppliers and customers are invited to clarify what is and is not working in achieving your desired level of excellence. Internal customers are asked for feedback on current levels of performance, and action plans for improved responsiveness are created.

Quality Steering Team (QST): A cross-section of organizational team members is commissioned to lead the continuous implementation and measurement of *your* quality improvement efforts -- in effect, to keep you on course with your improvement journey.

Leadership Development Lab (LDL): All key team members develop essential communication and leadership skills to maximize the effectiveness of the entire organization. Participants develop the insights, skills and abilities to empower everyone in the organization to peak performance.

Performance Team Lab (PTL): Everyone understands the purposes of performance teams and masters the skills and techniques that make teams successful. Teams learn effective problem-solving techniques and self-management methods to improve their processes and effectiveness, allowing for and encouraging continuous improvement.

Continuous Improvement Coaching (CIC): Sustaining your commitment to ongoing improvement. Planning and coaching in targeted areas where continuous improvement is desired, including customer service, sales, supervision, process improvement and problem-solving.

Turbo Sales System (TSS): This system turbo-charges your sales team's skills, heightens their motivation and increases organizational abilities. TSS dramatically improves sales effectiveness by experientially improving key interpersonal sales skills and developing a proven method of organization and accountability.

Superior Customer Service (SCS): Produces a transformation in which all team members approach their daily activities from the customer's point of view, resulting in greater cooperation and a positive approach to excellence and follow-through.

Managing Customer Relations (MCR): Designed to help your team develop and deliver "World-Class Service." Delivering superior, cost-effective service is the element that differentiates "World-Class" companies from their competitors.

Construction Partnering for Success (CPS): Partnering reframes and moves owners, contractors, engineers, and inspectors from confrontation to alliance -- a pledge of cooperation and teamwork.

TURBO 🌀
Leadership Systems

"Empowering your team to ensure continuous improvement."

36280 NE Wilsonville Rd.
Newberg, OR 97132
(503) 625-1867 / Fax: (503) 625-2699
www.turboleadershipsystems.com
turbo@turboleadershipsystems.com

Order Form

Please send me

___copies of *15 Leadership Principles & Ronald Reagan* @ $24.95 each

___copies of *Motorcycle Meditations* @ $19.95 each

___copies of *Making Moments Matter* @ $9.95

___copies of *In Formation* @ $19.95 each

___copies of *Empowering Leadership* @ $24.95

___copies of *Repeat Business* @ $9.95

___copies of *How To Turbo-Charge You* @ $14.95

___copies of *Communicating For Results* @ $ 9.95

___copies of *The Great Baseball Cap* @ $9.95

❒ Please send me at no charge complete information about the training services of Turbo Leadership Systems™.

Add $2.00 for shipping and handling for first item and $1.00 for each additional item, for a total amount of $_____.

❒ Check enclosed   ❒ Bill my MasterCard/VISA

Account #_____

Expires_____   Signature_____
Ship to
Name:_____

Company: _____

Address:_____

_____

City/State/Zip:_____

Phone:_____

Mail, e-mail or fax your order to:
Turbo Leadership Systems™
36280 N.E. Wilsonville Rd.
Newberg, Oregon 97132
Phone: (503) 625-1867 / Fax: (503) 625-2699
turbo@turboleadershipsystems.com

.